"Are you aw[...]
he breathed against her lips

Toni turned her head into Nick's broad shoulder, overwhelmed by deep regret. How could she have opened her heart to this man? She knew there was no future for her and Nick. Nor could there ever be.

"I must have had too much wine last night," she whispered. "Oh, Nick, what have I done?"

Nick smoothed tousled hair back from her face, then tilted her chin up to search her eyes. "You haven't knowingly done anything, sweetheart, and neither have I." Warm lips leisurely feathered her temple, moved lazily down to nuzzle her neck. "Give me today, Toni," he murmured. "I'm just selfish enough to think there's a solution to our problem . . . ."

Dear Reader,

We at Harlequin are extremely proud to introduce our new series, **HARLEQUIN TEMPTATION**. Romance publishing today is exciting, expanding and innovative. We have responded to the ever-changing demands of you, the reader, by creating this new, more sensuous series. Between the covers of each **HARLEQUIN TEMPTATION** you will find an irresistible story to stimulate your imagination and warm your heart.

Styles in romance change, and these highly sensuous stories may not be to every reader's taste. But Harlequin continues its commitment to satisfy all your romance-reading needs with books of the highest quality. Our sincerest wish is that **HARLEQUIN TEMPTATION** will bring you many hours of pleasurable reading.

THE EDITORS

U.S.
HARLEQUIN TEMPTATION
2504 WEST SOUTHERN AVE.
TEMPE, ARIZONA
85282

CAN.
HARLEQUIN TEMPTATION
P.O. BOX 2800
POSTAL STATION "A"
WILLOWDALE, ONTARIO
M2N 5T5

By Mutual Consent

MARION SMITH COLLINS

Harlequin Books

TORONTO • NEW YORK • LONDON
AMSTERDAM • PARIS • SYDNEY • HAMBURG
STOCKHOLM • ATHENS • TOKYO • MILAN

Published April 1984

ISBN 0-373-25105-X

Printed in Canada

1

A VOICE came over the loudspeaker. "Ladies and gentlemen, you will notice that the captain has illuminated the seat-belt sign. We are now on our final approach and will be landing in Atlanta in approximately ten minutes. Please extinguish all smoking materials and return your seat backs and trays to the upright position."

Antonia Grey stubbed out her cigarette in the tiny ashtray on the arm of her seat. She shifted slightly under the confinement of the seat belt and crossed her legs.

The man sitting next to her tilted his head slightly. His eyes traveled the length of her well-shaped calf and then raised to meet hers in an appreciative smile.

She met his gaze without rebuke, but with an impassive indifference that was much more quelling, and turned to look out the window. A solid thump vibrated through the seat beneath her, indicating that the landing gear was locked into place. Moments later, the wheels of the plane touched down. When the huge aircraft had finally come to a full stop, the soft voice of the flight attendant again came on the intercom to welcome them to Atlanta.

Toni didn't move except to remove her glasses with their tortoiseshell frames. She rested her head against the back of the seat and closed her eyes, twirling the glasses absently in her hand. Just a short respite, a few minutes, before she would have to get off the plane. She was so tired—bone weary. She dreaded the weekend and the caustic remarks that her stepmother relished as sophisticated banter. *I'm a changeling, I suppose,* she reflected fancifully. *Except that the fairies didn't spirit the beautiful child away before they brought me. They left both of us.*

All around her people were reaching for coats, hand luggage, magazines, and struggling into the aisles to move slowly along toward the exit. Why had she agreed to come home for such a short trip? She would be exhausted Monday after the round of parties this weekend.

"But it's your sister's engagement party!" her stepmother had admonished her over the telephone. "Angela will be crushed if you don't come. How can you be so selfish?"

"Agnes, I'm not being selfish! But I'm graduating in two months, and our professors have piled on the work," she pleaded.

"Pooh!" With one word Agnes carelessly dismissed all the work of seven years. Four years in undergraduate school and three years of law school—it had been a long hard grind, but soon she would have a law degree.

Agnes had never understood Toni's desire for a career. Her life consisted of a constant round of luncheons, teas, garden-club meetings, and shopping. She was well satisfied with it, and to give her credit, Agnes did a lot of volunteer work. The Atlanta Ballet and the High Museum of Art would probably fold if Agnes ever decided to cease her fund-raising activities. Angela would be satisfied, too, with that kind of life, but not Toni. It was a life of total dependency, and she didn't ever intend to be dependent on anyone.

Toni sighed and opened her eyes. For a fleeting moment, without the glasses, she looked defenseless and vulnerable. Then she replaced them, and once again became what she wanted to be, the self-possessed career woman. The dusty-blue eyes that looked out from behind the frames had perfect vision. Toni used the glasses as a shield. They were only one of the shields she used to hide the real Antonia Grey. Her tailored, beige wool suit minimized her curves, and her tawny blond mane was always pulled back into a severe bun. Any escaping tendril was ruthlessly tucked in. The thoughtful reserved demeanor was another shield to hide a shy young woman, determined not to give too much of herself lest she be left without a prop. Few people saw the other side of Toni, the mischievous fun-loving side. She was satisfied with her ability to suppress it.

If anyone had told her that the owlish shape of the tortoiseshell frames made her eyes look huge and innocent, or that the exposed curve of her neck was delicately sensitive, or that the appealing fullness of her lips was intriguing, Toni would have been incredulous. She wanted to present an aura of self-sufficiency; and that wasn't easy when you were only five foot two. For some reason, if you were tiny, it was difficult for anyone to take you seriously, and Toni wanted to be taken very seriously.

The man next to her had disappeared, and the crowd in the aisles was beginning to thin out.

Wearily Toni got to her feet. She looped the strap of her serviceable leather bag over her shoulder and reached into the overhead compartment for her heavy camel's hair coat. She had needed its warmth when she boarded the plane in Boston, but in the waning days of March, Atlanta would be well into spring.

When Toni emerged from the jet bridge she looked around bewilderedly. Perhaps she should have had someone meet her. The relatively new Atlanta International Airport was a marvel of efficiency—*they* said. She smiled to herself and her spirits rose a bit. That kind of thinking was unprofessional. The ever-present "they" were always ready and willing to be quoted as a source—except in her chosen field, which demanded specifics.

There was a bank of telephones on the far wall, and she hurried toward them. She walked gracefully, her back straight. The pleated skirt swept against her legs, which were long in proportion to her height, causing more than one second look from the men behind her. But Toni was unaware of their glances as she fumbled in her shoulder bag for a coin.

"Hello?"

"Angela? It's Toni. I just landed."

"Toni!" Her sister greeted her voice enthusiastically and Toni smiled. "Hurry up," Angela urged. "It's almost time to go."

"I know. That's why I called. You all go ahead without me. I'll have to get a cab, and then change when I get home. I came right from class."

"Oh, dear. Well, all right. We'll meet you at the club. You can bring my car. I'll leave the keys here."

"Okay! See you soon."

"Toni?" Her sister's voice softened. "Thanks for coming. I know you're awfully busy, but I need your moral support. You know Agnes," she drawled.

Toni laughed. "Oh, yes, I know Agnes! Bye."

There was nothing Agnes liked better than a "project," and Toni was sure that Angela's wedding would be a "project" in capital letters. Angela got along well with Agnes, but Toni didn't. In fact, Angela was well named. Good-natured, sympathetic and loving, she got along well with everyone.

Toni had tried to please her stepmother when she was living at home, but for some reason the older woman resented her and made it obvious. Toni had learned to live with the knowledge that they could never be close, but she still didn't understand why. Oh, well. . . . She shrugged slim shoulders and turned to join the moving crowd.

By following the arrows directing her to Baggage Pickup and a melodious recorded voice giving further directions, she made her way eventually to a cavern of a room where carousels belched luggage from somewhere deep in the bowels of the building. She dragged her heavy suitcase off a conveyor belt just before it was about to be swallowed up again in a menacing black hole covered with a flapping rubber curtain.

The few skycaps on duty all seemed to have their dollies well filled, so she manhandled the bag toward the exit herself. Angela would never have had to go through this! At the thought of her sister another small smile played about her generous mouth. Angela would have looked helpless and batted those long eyelashes, and ten men would have fought to carry her luggage. Toni's lashes were even longer than Angela's, but she had never been able to perfect the technique. Toni was the practical one, or as their stepmother loved to remind her, the brainy one; Angela, of course, was the beauty.

Toni stepped outside the building and looked for a taxi. Seeing one off to her left, she waved and the man eased his cab forward to where she was standing. He got out and came around to open the door for her. Grateful for this particularly Southern courtesy, she collapsed against the seat while he put her suitcase in the trunk. When he got back in he lowered the metal flag with a click and said, "Where to, lady?"

"Tuxedo Road, northwest," she answered.

"Right. Is this the first time you've flown into Atlanta?"

"No, but I never get used to it. How did you know?"

His black face split in a grin. "I recognize the bewildered look."

Toni grimaced. "The airport's like something out of 1984!"

The driver chuckled. "Even George Orwell wouldn't

have gone that far! Still, the passenger flow is smoother. Another couple of years and the old airport would have come to a dead halt."

"You sound very knowledgeable," Toni told him.

"I'm majoring in transportation engineering at Georgia Tech." He chuckled again. "I figure I'm getting my basic course by driving a cab at night."

The address she had given him was on the opposite side of the city from the airport, so even using the interstate highway to cut through traffic it was almost half an hour before he pulled into the circular driveway in front of the house.

Toni paid him, adding a generous tip, and thanked him with a smile when he deposited her suitcase at the front door. He drove off, whistling.

Toni stood for a moment looking at the white Georgian facade. Home... it was so beautiful. As she mounted the steps her arm brushed a trailing branch of a weeping cherry tree in full bloom. The movement released the heady scent of the flowers, and she paused in the twilight to savor the smell. She looked across the smooth expanse of lawn to banks of blooming azaleas in all shades of pink and, behind them, flowering pink dogwood trees. Sighing deeply as she drank in the sight, she thought there was just no place on earth to compare with the beauty of Atlanta in the spring.

The front door opened, spilling light over the flagstone steps and pinning Toni in its glare.

"Toni? I thought I heard a car. Why are you standing out here, child?"

Toni ran up the steps to throw her arms around

the ample figure. "Nervy! Oh, Nervy! It's so good to be home."

Plump arms folded lovingly around her. Minerva Davis had been nursemaid and substitute mother to the girls since Angela was four, and Toni, two, the year their own mother had died. Toni knew that Minerva, or Nervy as they called her, would give her the warmest welcome of her homecoming. For as long as Toni could remember, Nervy had been the only person who ever understood the serious, studious little girl.

Not until Angela and Toni were nine and seven respectively had their father married again. Agnes, their stepmother, had joined the ranks of relatives who doted on Angela, with her ethereal looks and sweet manner, and ignored Toni. Even then she had appeared to be an independent child. Only Nervy recognized the need in her—the need of a child who didn't remember the warmth and tenderness of a mother's embrace. Others assumed that because she was a quiet child she was content.

"Why don't you come home more often?" Nervy scolded gently.

"I'm busy, Nervy. And, well...."

"I know, I know, child," she comforted as she turned to lead Toni inside. She was a large woman. Toni was a full six inches shorter.

The gray streaks in Nervy's hair seemed wider than they had been when Toni was home for Christmas holidays. Her shoulders, too, were not quite as resolutely squared, and her voice sounded weary.

Toni's brows knitted in a frown. "Are you all right, Nervy? You don't look well."

The older woman sighed dismissively. "I'm just tired, child." Then she did straighten her shoulders, but the action appeared to take an effort.

Toni resolved to speak to Douglas before the weekend was over. Douglas was Nervy's husband. They lived in an apartment on one side of the house, and he was chauffeur-gardener-handyman for her father and Agnes. If anything were seriously wrong Nervy would never tell her, but she could get the truth from Douglas.

Nervy interrupted her thoughts. "I'm to hurry you on your way, Toni. Your call came later than your daddy expected, so they've gone on ahead to the party."

"Good! Then you can visit with me while I dress." She started dragging her case away from the door. "I want to hear all about this paragon that Angela has pulled from a hat!"

"Leave your suitcase. You go on upstairs, and I'll have Douglas bring it up."

"Thanks, Nervy." Toni started up the broad circular staircase. "Are you coming?"

"I'll be there in a minute." Nervy disappeared down a hallway to their right.

TONI STEPPED OUT OF THE SHOWER, refreshed. Her built-in store of energy was almost up to its normal level. She wrapped herself in a large bath sheet and reentered her bedroom.

Nervy was unpacking her suitcase and chuckling at the extravagant bits of lace and silk. "No one looking at the way you dress would ever guess that under the tailored suits, you wear things like this!"

Toni grinned at her. "They're my concession to femininity, Nervy, and I love them," she said. She lifted panties and a bra from the pile in Nervy's arms.

Nervy gave a snort. "Concession, my foot!" she said. "There's no way you can hide your femininity, child. I don't care how you fix your hair or what kind of clothes you wear."

"Well, I should hope not! I don't want to look like a man. But, Nervy, no one would have confidence in my ability as a lawyer if I wore sexy clothes on the outside—so I wear them inside instead!" She laughed and went to the closet to take down a silk jersey dress of royal blue.

"And Angela is just the opposite! In spite of what Mrs. Grey says, I believe it's really your sister who's the practical one." Nervy deposited the lacy underwear in a drawer and came over to zip Toni's dress. "No one will mistake you for a boy in this one anyway." The dress was a long, pencil-thin sheath with a gracefully draped cowl neck. "That hem is a tad longer than you usually wear them. You be careful not to trip on it!" she warned.

Toni giggled. "I hope I've outgrown my awkward stage, Nervy. Why, I haven't fallen on my face in months!"

The older woman met her smile in the mirror.

Toni was the child who came home with scraped knees and sprained ankles. Her boundless energy always ran ahead of her physical coordination, but now she had grown into a truly graceful and poised young woman.

Toni turned, surveying her reflection. She smoothed the silky material over her hips. "I've never worn this dress before. Do you think it clings too much?"

"Of course not!" Nervy snorted. "Honestly, Toni, you've got to get over this fixation of yours about looking like an attractive woman!"

"I know, but it's been drummed into my brain for three years that I'm going to be a woman competing in a man's world."

"I thought that kind of idea went out with women's liberation."

"Well, the opportunities are better than they were. But the professors still seem to think that women are only in the profession temporarily, until they start a family."

"And you? How do you feel about that? Are you going to leave your children with a nurse?"

Toni laughed. "I'm a long way from having to worry about that, Nervy. I haven't met a man yet that I could be more than mildly interested in!"

"Someday you will."

"Well, 'someday' is a long way off. Now, tell me about this Nicholas Trabert," said Toni, referring to her sister's fiancé. "What's he like?" She sat down at the dressing table.

Nervy pondered a moment. "Well, I like him. He's

certainly handsome enough. He's the dark-and-devil-may-care type. He and Angela make a striking couple. She's so fair." She hesitated, and Toni sensed that there was more she wanted to say.

"What is it, Nervy? Is something wrong?" The hand holding the mascara brush stopped in midair.

"I don't quite know how to say it. It's just that somehow something is missing. There's no spark between them. For an engaged couple they seem, well...remarkably patient. And you get the idea that Nick isn't a patient man. In fact, just the opposite. I think he'd be fiercely jealous and possessive of someone he really loved."

"You mean you don't think he loves Angela?" Toni was shocked.

"No, not that, exactly." She paused. "He obviously loves her. How could anyone not love her?" Nervy asked with a smile.

"I know. She is a darling!" Toni had always been extremely protective of her sister. Though Angela was two years older than Toni, she seemed to be the one who needed taking care of.

"Nick seems to love Angela more as we love her—like a sister, or a daughter." She laughed a little self-consciously. "I guess what I'm trying to say is that I look for a few banked fires, and there aren't any. They're like two very good friends. He's a lucky man! No one would deny that. Angela will make a wonderful wife. I just hope your stepmother hasn't pushed her into something she's not ready for. She kept telling her that at twenty-six she should be looking for a husband. So Angela seems to have just reached out and plucked the most suitable one she could find to keep Mrs. Grey from harassing her any longer. And he is very suitable. Handsome, wealthy and successful. What more could a girl want? Oh, well. I guess I'm just being capricious. And you'd better get dressed!" She picked up the beige suit coat from the bed and draped it on a padded hanger. "Maybe Angela will talk to you," she added absently.

Toni skipped lightly down the stairs, still talking to Nervy who stood on the landing above. Her head was turned, looking back and up, and so she was unaware of the man who had entered the hall from the living room.

She saw Nervy smile over her shoulder and her head snapped around, but it was too late. Her forward impetus could not be stopped, and losing her balance on the last step, she careered into him. Strong arms came around her waist as he fought for his footing on the highly polished floor, but she overbalanced him and they both went crashing to the floor, Toni on top.

The force of the fall knocked Toni's glasses from her nose. They went skittering across the tiled floor. Her smooth chignon was dislodged, and the tawny curtain of hair spilled around her face.

Too stunned to move for a moment, Toni looked down into the blackest eyes she'd ever seen. They roamed over her face in warm appraisal, then narrowed as they met hers. Shaken by more than the fall, she couldn't seem to tear her gaze away. She caught her lower lip between her teeth, and his dark eyes followed the motion. "Are... are you all right?" she asked in a small voice.

He watched her lips as she spoke. She could feel the strong heartbeat in his chest. He lifted his head a fraction of an inch toward her mouth. Then he seemed to recall himself. He dragged his eyes back up to meet hers and smiled. 'Why don't we get up and I'll see?" he said in a deep vibrant voice. The even white teeth contrasted engagingly with his tan, and Toni caught her breath. He was alarmingly handsome.

Suddenly Toni realized the intimacy of their positions. Her hands were on his broad shoulders, and her breasts were crushed against a powerful chest. Her face was only inches away from that sensual mouth. Muscular thighs were entangled with her legs. Awkwardly she scrambled to her feet and he came up with her, a steadying hand at her waist. She looked up into his eyes.

He seemed to hold his breath for a moment. His dark eyes probed hers. Her heart was pounding erratically, and Toni didn't know whether it was from the fall or from the virility of this tall man. She swallowed the lump in her throat and murmured, "I'm really very sorry."

His hand tightened at her waist. The encounter had lasted only for a short minute, but his touch was almost familiar. Unconsciously she swayed toward him.

"Toni! Are you all right?" Nervy had reached the bottom of the steps.

With an effort Toni turned away from the man. "I'm fine, Nervy." Her voice shook slightly in reaction to his nearness.

Nervy looked beyond her. "And you, Nick?"

Toni whirled. "You're Nick?"

The hand at her waist dropped. He smiled strangely and nodded. "And you're Toni," he said, his voice heavy.

"Oh, no!" Toni whispered.

Nervy looked at her in surprise. "Why, Toni!" she admonished.

Toni had never been so unnerved, and it had nothing to do with the fall. Her hand went to her temple. "I...I mean...what a horrible way for us to meet!" she improvised. "My glasses!" She looked around the floor frantically. "Oh, I hope they aren't broken!"

The glasses were under a table and Nick retrieved them for her. He held them up. "They're not broken," he said, looking through the lenses. Then his eyes narrowed, and he brought them closer to his face. He looked at Toni speculatively as he held them out to her.

"Thank you! I'm so relieved. I don't have a spare pair with me " She took them from him and slipped them onto her nose

"I should think not," Nick said teasingly, and Toni's eyes flew to his face.

He studied her, a crease between his eyebrows.

"What are you doing here, Nick?" asked Nervy.

"I came back to pick up Toni. Angela was worried about her coming alone. And we'd better get going." He shot back his cuff to look at a slim gold watch on his wrist.

At the mention of her sister's name, Toni felt a warm flush steal upward into her face. She tried to be casual as she said, "Yes. Just let me run upstairs and fix my hair."

His eyes ranged over the tawny gold. "Your hair looks fine to me."

Toni ignored his remark. She had already started up the steps. "It won't take a minute."

When she reached the sanctuary of her room she closed the door and leaned against it. She needed this moment or two to regain her composure. What was wrong with her? Her body was still warm and strangely awake where it had touched his. She groaned aloud and made her shaking legs take her to the dressing table, her shaking hand pick up the brush. It was just an ordinary reaction to an extremely virile masculine man, she told herself. A man who, incidentally, was her sister's fiancé!

When she descended the stairs a few minutes later her equanimity was restored—a bit unstable, but in place.

Nervy and Nick still stood where she had left them, talking seriously in undertones. Toni had a chance to watch them unobserved. Nick's arm rested lightly on the doorframe above Nervy's head. His other hand was in the pocket of his tuxedo pants. The stance pulled his white silk shirtfront taut across his broad chest. He must be well over six feet tall, with the body of an athlete and the demeanor of a very self-confident man. There was a stubborn thrust to his square jaw, but laugh lines radiated from the corners of his eyes. He was a man used to having his way, dynamic and forceful, from the self-assured carriage of his body to the slightly arrogant tilt of his head.

Nick was the first to see her. His eyes skimmed over her and his brows came together in a frown, but he didn't say anything as he took the white mohair jacket that she carried and put it over her shoulders.

Toni felt his fingers linger there, and then she moved quickly toward the older woman. "Good-night, Nervy," she said, kissing her. "I'll see you in the morning!"

"Good night, honey. Have a good time." Nervy stood at the door watching them as they drove away. There was a puzzled look on her face.

Mercifully, they had to travel only a few blocks to reach the clubhouse where her parents were giving the party. As Nick pulled out of the driveway, Toni said brightly, "Angela tells me you're a lawyer."

"That's right. And you're almost one?" That deep resonant voice sent fresh chills down her spine.

"Two more months! If I survive," she answered a little breathlessly.

He chuckled. "You'll survive. You know, twelve years ago I probably sat in your chair and thought the same thing. The professors try to make that last six months as difficult as possible."

Toni finally allowed herself to glance sideways at his profile. His smile had deepened the furrows on his tanned cheeks. The planes of his face were strong. Raven-black hair brushed the collar of his dinner jacket, which looked as though it had been tailored to fit the broad shoulders. Her eyes were drawn to his hands on the steering wheel, and she remembered his touch. She jerked her head around to face the front. This would not do!

"Are you in Professor Winter's contracts class?" Nick asked.

Her mind had been so far from law school that she was blank for a moment. "Yes! Yes, I am."

"Then I'll be seeing you in two weeks."

"Wha—at?" She swiveled her head to meet his laughing eyes.

"I have to be in Boston on business the first week in April, and he's invited me to speak to his classes."

Toni was astounded. "Then you must really be an expert!"

Nick chuckled. "Hardly." He turned into the long driveway of the club.

The beautiful building had at one time been a private residence, surrounded by extensive grounds. He pulled the car to a halt under a stone porte cochere, where a parking attendant opened Toni's door.

Nick came around the car to join her before he answered. "Not an expert," he said. "I'm not sure there could ever be an expert in contract law. Each situation is so completely different from the last. Necessity has forced me to learn as much about the subject as possible. I speak on it at bar-association meetings occasionally."

"It's my favorite class, and I know what you mean about each contract being different. I find it very challenging." She was impressed. Despite his denial she knew that Professor Winter wasn't one to give his class over to less than an expert in the field. "I'll look forward to hearing you."

"I don't know that I'll be at my best with you in the class," Nick said, reaching in front of her for the brass door handle.

Toni looked sharply at him, but he didn't meet her eyes. Instead he took her jacket and gave it to the coatroom attendant. Taking her arm he said, "I hope you'll have dinner with me while I'm in Boston." They mounted the three steps to the great hall, which was deserted at the moment. The jewellike colors of Oriental rugs softened the stone floors.

Toni didn't answer his invitation. The only sound was their footsteps, alternately echoing on stone and muffled by rugs. She looked down at the tiny beaded bag in her hands, hiding her expression. Having dinner with her sister's fiancé was innocent enough— except when that fiancé had such a riotous effect on her own senses.

"Well?" he asked.

"I...I may be busy," she answered. Her voice was a little husky. "Things are very hectic right now."

"Toni...." He started to say something, but she hurried ahead of him into what had once been the library of the beautiful home. Rich wood paneling adorned the walls. Blue velvet love seats flanked the fireplace, and soft lights warmed the room.

The party had gathered here for predinner drinks, and Toni scanned the crowd for the blond head of her sister. She saw her across the room and started to move toward her.

At that moment Angela turned and spotted her. "Toni! At last!" Angela rushed over, and Toni returned her embrace with a warm desperation.

"I thought you'd never get here?" She smiled at her fiancé. "Thanks, Nick." Then she held Toni away and surveyed her. "Darling, you're so pale! Too much time in those stuffy old classrooms!"

Toni gave her sister a warm smile. "Probably. But it won't be for much longer!"

A waiter approached with a tray of champagne glasses. Toni took one gratefully and sipped the golden liquid. "You look wonderful, Angela," she said.

Her sister did look wonderful. The salmon-colored chiffon dress was deceptively simple. It left Angela's lightly suntanned shoulders bare and billowed from the fitted bodice to swirl around her ankles. A halo of soft golden curls framed her heart-shaped face. Her eyes were the same clear beguiling blue as Toni's.

"Doesn't she though? Being engaged agrees with her!" A hearty voice spoke from behind Toni.

Toni was still looking at Angela, and at their father's words she saw a slight cloud pass over Angela's face. "Hello, daddy," she murmured as she turned to kiss him.

"Hello, Toni. I'm glad Agnes talked you into coming. After all, it isn't every day your sister gets engaged."

"No, it certainly isn't!" Toni answered promptly. *And it isn't every day your daughter graduates from law school, either. I wonder if Agnes will let you come to that,* she speculated as she looked up at her handsome silver-haired father.

Nick put voice to her thoughts. "I suppose you'll all be going to Boston for Toni's graduation. It isn't every day your daughter graduates cum laude from law school, either."

Toni's eyes met the amused gleam in his with a shocked stare. Could he read her mind? And how did he know about the cum laude? The list hadn't been published.

"Of course we are!" Angela exclaimed. "Toni, you didn't tell me about graduating with honors!"

Toni very carefully set her champagne glass down. Her hands had begun to tremble, and her eyes behind the owlish lenses were bright. "I didn't know! It hasn't been announced yet. Are you sure?" she asked Nick, afraid to believe.

"I'm sure. Professor Winter told me." He smiled down at her. "Congratulations."

Toni clasped her hands together under her chin. "I can't believe it!" Her face glowed.

"Well, I think it's wonderful! I'm so proud of my little sister!" Angela linked her arm with Toni's.

Their stepmother approached the group and presented a cheek, which Toni dutifully kissed. Agnes was lovely in a gown of ice-blue chiffon. Her silver hair curved toward her face in an artlessly casual style that must have meant hours at the hairdresser's. "What are you so proud of, Angela?" she asked.

"Toni's graduating with honors, Agnes! Isn't that marvelous? I can't wait to see her!"

"Oh, dear! I had meant to tell you!" Agnes's voice was regretful. "The Adlers want to give a party for you and Nick that weekend. They're going abroad for the summer, and it's the only time they have." She laid a cool hand on Toni's arm. "I'm sure you understand, Toni. The Adlers are such close friends. They would be devastated if they couldn't entertain for these young people!"

A deathly silence greeted her words. Toni lifted her head proudly, and she forced a calm tone into her voice when she said, "Certainly, Agnes."

Daniel Grey cleared his throat. "Agnes, you should have checked with me before you accepted. I'm not sure—"

Agnes interrupted, "But I did check the date— with both you and Angela!"

"Well, when you asked me I guess I didn't realize it was the weekend of Toni's graduation. The party will just have to be changed," said Angela firmly.

"We'll see," said Agnes, a self-satisfied smile on her face. "Let's not argue about it here. This is a party! Have you seen Angela's ring, Toni?"

Angela held out her hand a little reluctantly, and Toni absently admired the diamond, trying to ignore the large obstruction in her throat.

Agnes began to shepherd everyone toward the dining room. "Shall we go in to dinner?" she said gaily.

Nick hadn't said a word during the exchange, but as Agnes moved away he put a comforting hand on Toni's shoulder. She caught a glimpse of sympathy in his eyes and shrugged off his touch with a dark scowl.

2

EXCEPT FOR ANGELA AND NICK, the family members were dispersed. Each one of them was host at a table for eight. White napery gleamed in the candlelight. In the center of each round table was a spring arrangement of jonquils, irises and tulips. Toni's table consisted mainly of friends of her late grandmother, and she was relieved. At least she wouldn't have to make small talk with people she didn't know.

Why on earth did Agnes hate her so? For hatred was the emotion that she had seen gleaming out of her eyes that night. There was no mistaking it. For years Toni had known that her stepmother preferred Angela. She had always assumed that it was because they were very much alike, but that couldn't possibly account for her malice. Her stepmother wasn't just thoughtlessly selfish—she really hated her. And Toni could think of no earthly reason that she should.

Many incidents swam to the surface of her mind as she smiled and made light conversation with the people at her table. Some of the memories were painful; some, almost comical.

From across the table Mrs. Mallory asked a question about law school. Toni murmured a polite answer.

Then Brigadier General Paxton Norwood III, on her left, began a discourse on his favorite subject—military spending—with Senator Robert Charles, on her right, freeing her attention. She allowed her thoughts to drift back....

IT WAS A SCHOOL HOLIDAY and the circus was in town. Each year the parents' organization at their school rented buses to take the third-grade students into the city for the performance. Two years before a tearful Toni had bitten her lip as she'd watched Angela leave for the outing. Afterward they had sat up half the night while Toni listened, wide-eyed, to the tales of elephants and tigers, and girls in spangled costumes flying through the air.

This year she was in the third grade and it was her turn. From her lofty maturity of eleven years, an indulgent Angela had again relived every exciting moment of her circus trip for nine-year-old Toni.

At breakfast that morning Agnes was impatient with them. "For heaven's sake, can't you two be quiet? We've heard nothing this entire week except 'circus'! And I am heartily bored by the subject."

"Yes, Agnes. We're sorry." Angela apologized for them both, but there was a twinkle in her eye as she glanced over at Toni.

Toni's heart, which had begun to pound at Agnes's harsh words, suddenly felt warm again. Angela was the best sister in the whole world.

Excusing herself, she left the table and raced upstairs to dress. Agnes had grudgingly agreed when Toni asked for permission to wear her jeans today. Their stepmother considered jeans far too casual and rarely let the girls leave the house in them.

Toni was dressed and scrambling around on the floor of her closet for her shoes when Angela called from downstairs.

"Toni! Your ride is here!

She came up with one tasseled loafer in her hand. Where was her other shoe? Frantically she began to throw footwear over her head. Summer sandals, outgrown sneakers, ballet slippers—hardly worn—sailed through the air. Oh, why hadn't she cleaned out her closet as Agnes had told her to? Finally, in desperation, she reached for her black patent-leather Sunday shoes and buckled them on. Her fingers trembled in haste. When she jumped up to leave the room she was suddenly confronted with Agnes, standing in the door of her room like a forbidding chancellor.

Hands planted on her hips, her stepmother took in the chaos of the room with a dark frown. "What is the meaning of this?" she demanded. There was an expression on her face that could almost have been satisfaction.

"I can only find one shoe," Toni wailed. "I don't know *where* the other one is!"

"I'm not surprised," Agnes said sarcastically. "Well, you are not going to prance around the circus grounds in your new shoes! Take them off."

"Maybe Nervy can help me find them." Toni started to get up but was stopped by her stepmother's forbidding tone.

"Minerva is in the kitchen. Take those shoes off," she repeated, enunciating each word in a cold voice.

"But, Agnes—"

"You heard me," Agnes said sternly. "If you aren't downstairs in three minutes, *in* the proper shoes, I shall tell them to go on without you."

"No! Agnes, please..." Toni protested to an empty doorway. She hesitated for only a fraction of a second before diving into the closet again, upsetting tennis rackets and upending a box of out-of-season clothes.

Angela had heard the uproar and came in to help. "Toni, where could it be?" She sounded almost as frantic as Toni felt. "Under the bed!" Her sister threw aside the comforter to look. "No, it's not there," she moaned. She sat on her heels and looked around helplessly.

The sound of a car ignition reached their ears. A powerful engine purred and slowly, almost reluctantly, accelerated.

Toni's huge blue eyes were unbelieving as they met the despairing sympathy in Angela's. She leaped to her feet and ran to the window. As she watched, her feet rooted to the floor, a large black car turned out of the driveway onto the street with what seemed like heartrending finality to her. The brake lights blinked once as though in regretful farewell.

Toni felt a throbbing in her temples and tears began to scald her eyes. Slowly, very slowly, she turned. There was a burning obstruction in her throat. Angela stood up and came toward her.

"Why . . . ?" she croaked, looking to her older sister for an answer that Angela couldn't provide.

Empathetic tears spilled from Angela's eyes. "I don't know, Toni," she whispered. "I don't know."

Toni's small body collapsed in her sister's arms, racked with deep pitiful sobs.

"DON'T YOU AGREE, Toni?" General Norwood's question broke through into her consciousness.

"Of course," she murmured huskily, wondering vaguely what she had agreed to. She had been so far away, so lost in the memory, that it was an effort to recall herself to the present. It wasn't the tragedy she'd considered it at the time—there had been other circuses—but never one as important to a nine-year-old girl. Over the years other confrontations with Agnes had not ended so unhappily. Her dimple deepened as she recalled the rock concert when she was sixteen.

Her current boyfriend had stood in line all night to get two tickets, which he had presented to Toni with the air of a conqueror. "We're in the second row!"

Unfortunately Agnes and her father had walked into the room at that moment. "Do you really intend to let your daughter be exposed to all those hippies and drug addicts?" Agnes asked her husband in a frosty voice.

Daniel had winked at the young man. "I just wish

you'd gotten four tickets. I wouldn't mind hearing that group myself.''

On that occasion Agnes had left the room in a huff.

After dinner the toasts were drunk and a combo tuned up for dancing. Lights dimmed and the newly engaged couple moved onto the floor in the glare of a spotlight. They danced well together. Angela was so graceful, and Nick, with his dark good looks, was a perfect foil for her blond beauty. After a chorus the spotlight was turned off, and other couples joined them on the floor.

Her father came over to claim Toni for the dance. ''I don't know why Agnes didn't put some young people at your table,'' he grumbled.

Toni didn't answer. There wouldn't have been any point. Instead she looked up at him. The silver-gray hair was brushed away from his temples with a slight wave. His face was tanned and healthy, and his blue eyes, slightly troubled now, were nevertheless good-humored. ''You're the best-looking man here. Do you know that?''

He laughed, causing several people to look at them. ''You are good for an old man's ego!''

Toni snorted. ''Old man, my eye!''

His face sobered. ''Sometimes I feel old. One daughter engaged, and my baby about to embark on a career—yes, sometimes I feel very old.''

''Daddy, don't!'' Toni choked.

Daniel Grey looked down at his daughter. ''Toni, I have to talk to you,'' he said. ''But not here. Let's go out to the terrace for a minute.''

Toni led the way around the dancing couples to the French doors on the far side of the room. When they were outside, she breathed a deep sigh of relief. "That's better. It was getting stuffy in there."

Her father lit a cigarette and stood for a moment looking out into the darkness.

"May I have one?"

He looked at her sharply. "I didn't know you smoked," he said, holding out the package to her.

"Only in times of extreme stress," she said lightly as she put the cigarette to her lips. Daniel flicked a gold lighter and held it to the tip. Toni inhaled. "I have a feeling this is one of those times."

"I hope not," her father said wryly. "I thought I owed you an explanation for Agnes's behavior."

"Daddy, you don't have to—" Toni protested.

"Yes, I do," he interrupted. "I'm afraid I didn't realize how badly things have gotten out of hand. I'll admit it's mainly my fault. But to imply that a party is more important than your graduation...! That's pushing too far! I don't know what could have possibly gotten into Agnes."

"Why doesn't she like me?" Toni asked. Her voice was calm, almost indifferent, but inside she was churning with dread at where this conversation might lead. An uncomfortable premonition grew.

He flipped his cigarette over the low wall and pushed his hands into his pockets. He didn't answer for a long time. He seemed to be garnering his thoughts. Finally he spoke. "Because, Toni, the older you get, the more like your mother you are." He turned to look at her and his expression softened. "You could be her twin."

"Am I really? I mean...I've seen the pictures, but I wasn't sure...." With a jerky motion she put out her cigarette in a nearby ashtray. A formal portrait of her mother still hung in the dining room of the house on Tuxedo Road. Toni and Angela were grateful that their mother hadn't been consigned to the attic.... Suddenly Tony realized how awful it must be for Agnes to have to look at that portrait every evening.

She returned her attention to her father who was continuing in a tired voice, "Yes, you really are. I'm very proud of you, you know." His arm came around her shoulders, and they began to stroll slowly along the patio. "I may not tell you as often as I should, but I am. You and Angela are everything your mother and I hoped you would be."

She reached on tiptoe to plant a kiss on his cheek. "I'm very proud, too, of my handsome distinguished father."

Daniel's arm tightened for a moment before he let go of her to slide his hands back into his pockets. "Anyway, that's why Agnes is jealous." He hesitated before he continued. "Did you know that Agnes and I dated before I met your mother?"

"No!"

"We did. And I guess she expected...." His voice trailed off. "But the minute I met your mother that was it for me. I adored her, Toni. When she died, I died a little bit, too. No one could ever take her place. It seems like only yesterday...and again, it seems like another lifetime." He paused and cleared his throat. "I would never have married again, but when you and Angela were approaching your teenage years, I realized that Minerva and I weren't enough. You needed a mother. Agnes has given me companionship and all her love, even though she always knew that she was second in my heart."

Toni was quiet for a moment. Because of an accident of facial structure Agnes had always resented her. What irony! Always empathetic, Toni could suddenly put herself into Agnes's place, could feel what she felt. How very unhappy she must have been! Toni's resolve not to let someone ever become so important to her and cloud her emotions that thoroughly was strengthened.

She straightened her shoulders resolutely and turned to face her father. "Thank you for telling me this. It makes it easier to understand."

Daniel looked at her steadily. "I've come to realize that it was weak of me not to put my foot down with Agnes before this. I hope you'll be able to forgive me for not recognizing how bad the situation had become. I guess I felt guilty about Agnes—taking so much from her, never giving...but, Toni, we'll be at your graduation. I promise you that."

"Thank you," she whispered. "I really do want you to be there." Strangely, the only sorrow she felt was for the quiet, solemn little girl who had grown up on the periphery of her family and never understood why. Toni thought for a moment and then she cut the final cord, said the words that she knew would widen the breach between her and her family even more. "Daddy, will you do something for me?"

"What do you want me to do?"

Toni laid her hand on his arm. "Put my mother to rest. Let go of her. Move her portrait to one of the guest rooms." She felt the tensing of muscles under her hand and went on hurriedly, "You're too young to live with a ghost. If I am like my mother, I know she wouldn't have wanted you to. Agnes loves you. Give her a chance to share your life."

He looked at her, his eyes tender. His hand came up to touch her nose playfully. "Who is the parent here, and who is the child?" he asked.

"Angela is engaged. I'll soon have my own career. We'll be all right, so now is the time for the two of you to start thinking about yourselves," she urged.

Daniel sighed. "You're a remarkably generous girl, Toni." His hand covered hers on his arm. "Perhaps you're right. It's time I started giving."

"You'll be happier, daddy. I know you will." She managed a wide smile. "Well, as Agnes says 'this is a party!' Shall we go in?"

When Toni and Daniel reentered the club arm in arm three people watched them with interest—Nick and Angela from the dance floor, and Agnes from her table where she was sitting with the Adlers.

"Ask Agnes to dance," Toni urged her father in a whisper. "I'll entertain the Adlers." They approached the table.

"My dear, would you care to dance?" Daniel held

out his hand to Agnes and she put hers into it. There was a look in her eyes that saddened Toni. Why had she never noticed the uncertainty there? Agnes was grateful for the tiniest courtesy from her husband.

They left the table, and Toni slid into the seat Agnes had vacated. "Agnes says that you're going abroad for the summer. Tell me about your trip," Toni said with a smile. She listened with only half an ear as Mr. Adler began to describe their itinerary through Europe and the Middle East, but she nodded and made the right responses. "I may see you over there," she told him. "I've promised myself a vacation after graduation."

"Really, Toni? Where are you going?" Mrs. Adler asked.

"I haven't decided yet. I thought I'd like to rent a car and ramble. I've never been to Italy or Greece, and the Middle Eastern countries sound intriguing."

"Toni! You wouldn't go there by yourself, would you?" Angela's voice came from behind her.

Toni swiveled in her chair and met her sister's horrified eyes with a grin. "Why not? I can take care of myself," she said saucily.

Nick was frowning over Angela's shoulder. "That's a damned-foolish attitude!" he said stiffly.

Toni looked up at him, startled at his tone, and Angela's eyes widened in surprise. "Well, Nick, Toni has always been independent."

"That's no excuse for a lack of common sense. A girl alone in some of those countries would be asking for trouble."

Anger flashed from Toni's eyes, but she forced herself to remain silent and composed.

Nick seemed to sense the struggle that was going on inside her, for suddenly his face cleared and he said with amusement, "No comment?"

Toni lifted her chin but didn't answer.

"Then, may I have the pleasure of this dance, Miss Grey?" He held out a hand.

Toni glanced at Angela, but she was deep in conversation with the Adlers. Reluctantly she put her small hand in his big one. His fingers closed over hers with a warmth that tingled quickly up her arm.

The handkerchief-sized dance floor was crowded, which necessitated Nick's holding her close to the hard length of his body. His hand at her back was sending little signals to her nerve ends, waking them, making her feel more alive than she had ever felt.

What on earth was happening to her, she thought. Whatever it was, it was disturbing. She had never experienced an instant attraction to any man, and to feel it for Nick Trabert was impossible! She shifted away and his arm obligingly loosened, but she was still very much aware of him. She tried to hold herself rigid as they danced silently for a few minutes.

"Relax," Nick said, then added, "Where do you plan to practice law?"

She had to tilt her head back to meet the fathomless black eyes. "I—I'm not sure yet."

"With your record I'm sure you've had quite a few offers." He held her eyes with his.

"Some," she acknowledged automatically, but the effect of his gaze thickened her voice. "There is a firm in Baltimore that I like very much, or I may stay in Boston."

"You said you found contract law challenging, and John Winter certainly speaks highly of your ability. Would you like to work for me?"

She was stunned by the way her heart jumped at his suggestion.

"I'm not just offering, you know," he went on. "I plan to take in two more lawyers this year."

She was quiet for a long moment. The opportunity he was presenting her was one that yesterday she would have accepted without hesitation. "No," she answered at last. Her eyes fell to his black tie. "No, I don't think that would be a good idea." His warm breath on her temple was having an unruly effect on her pulse rate, and she pulled farther away from him.

"Why not?"

"Well...too much family togetherness, I guess." *And you're much too appealing for my peace of mind,* she added silently.

"You may be right." He dropped the subject and switched to another, one that was even more disagreeable. "You're an innocent child, aren't you, Toni?"

She stiffened. "I'll soon be twenty-five years old. Hardly a child," she said, deliberately keeping any defensive note from her voice.

"But innocent?"

"That depends on what you mean by innocent.

But it's hardly any of your business, is it?'' she asked, frowning. Her chin lifted and she looked at him. Her expression was more calm than she felt.

He ignored her question. "I'm curious. Have you ever been in love?"

Toni's eyes flashed with spirit. Suddenly she was angry. "I don't like personal questions, Mr. Trabert. I want to go back to my table, please." She started to pull away, but his arms tightened.

"Answer me!" he demanded huskily.

She felt the length of his long legs pressed against hers, and the sensation was a shock. "No, I've never been in love. I haven't had time. Does that answer your question?" she snapped. Toni wanted to jerk free, but looking around she knew that that would cause some raised eyebrows.

There was a smile of approval on his face. "More or less. But you can't take that trip alone, you know."

"What do you mean, I *can't* take the trip? I'll go if I want to!" she declared.

"We'll see," he answered enigmatically.

The music ended at that moment, and Toni slipped out of his arms with a swirl of blue silk jersey, grateful for the space between them. His nearness was something she couldn't tolerate for long, she admitted to herself.

"WHAT DID NICK SAY to put you on your high horse, Toni?" Angela asked. Tugging a comb through her light blond curls, she met Toni's startled eyes in the mirror of the ladies' lounge.

"Oh, nothing important. I shouldn't have let him upset me. He just doesn't think I should take the trip this summer," Toni answered with studied casualness.

"There seems to be a bit of a strain in the atmosphere between you two. I've never heard Nick criticize anyone before. Maybe he's attracted to you," she said idly.

"Angela! You're talking about your fiancé," Toni admonished. "Besides, that's ridiculous!"

"Is it?"

Toni searched her sister's face for resentment or jealousy, but there was none. Was this what Nervy meant? How could Angela treat a subject like this with such indifference? "Don't be silly, Angela," she remonstrated and breathed a sigh of relief when Angela seemed content to let the subject drop. The older sister replaced her comb into a gold evening bag and turned to watch Toni freshen the strawberry gloss on her lips, but when she spoke again Toni realized that she was determined to delve deeper.

"What do you think of Nick?" she asked.

Toni hesitated. "I think you're a very lucky girl," she said softly. "He's a handsome, successful, exciting man."

"Exciting? Really?" Angela seemed surprised. "Funny...that's the last word I would have used to describe Nick. He's always so serious."

"Angela, is anything wrong?" Toni faced her sister.

Angela was quiet for a minute. "I don't know. I

just thought that I'd feel differently when I became engaged, I guess. I thought I'd be tingly all over when he touched me. That I'd be miserable when we're apart. That I'd know his thoughts and feelings before he voiced them. But it isn't like that, Toni. Nick is kind and considerate, and a wonderful person, but I'm beginning to doubt my own feelings," she admitted. Her eyes were troubled. "Agnes says that I'm just living in a world of romantic novels." She smiled a little wistfully, which made Toni wonder. "She keeps telling me to grow up." Her fingers played restlessly with the clasp of her bag. "The only job I've ever had is the part-time modeling I do. She says that it's time for me to marry and 'take my place in society.'" There was a thread of hysteria in her voice as she mocked perfectly their stepmother's tone.

"It's the kind of life you've always wanted," Toni reminded gently.

Angela shrugged. "I thought so, but Agnes keeps pushing me to set a date."

Agnes? Not Nick? Toni thought that was strange.

"You know, Toni, she's a very unhappy person," Angela added.

Toni was grateful for the change of subject. "I know," she answered. "Maybe now that we're both going to be on our own, she and daddy will have more time for each other."

Toni wanted to warn her sister not to let Agnes push her into an engagement if she wasn't sure, but with her own reaction to Nick she decided that would be hypocritical. She kept her mouth firmly shut, and the moment passed when the warning would have seemed natural.

The girls left the lounge together. "Angela, if you don't mind, I'll catch a ride home with one of grandmother's friends."

"But, Toni! It's early yet!"

"I know, but I really am exhausted. Let me catch up on my rest tonight, and I'll take you on for tennis in the morning," Toni offered.

"You've got a game! Good night, little sister." Angela kissed her. "And thanks again for coming. I really did need you," she murmured, a sad smile marring her lovely features.

As Toni undressed for bed she wondered about the sadness in her sister's face.

3

"Deuce!" Angela called out from the other side of the net. The pleats of her white tennis dress swirled above long tanned legs as she prepared to serve.

Toni gripped her racket with hands that were wet with perspiration. Her own white cotton shorts and yellow-banded white tunic top were sticking to her. Angela had run her all over the court today. Usually they were evenly matched. The ball whizzed toward her, and she returned it with difficulty. Angela's backhand placed the ball just inside the line behind Toni.

"You've been practicing!" Toni accused breathlessly.

"My ad! No, you're just rusty! Hi, Nick!" Angela greeted her fiancé as he came through the gate behind Toni.

Toni's head jerked around.

Nick was dressed in plaid madras slacks, and a yellow knit shirt that stretched to cover the broad shoulders and muscular arms. "Who's winning?" he asked with a grin.

Toni's stomach knotted at the sight of his flashing white teeth. He sat on a bench with his long legs stretched lazily out in front of him, one arm casually hooked over the backrest. His air of masculinity was enhanced by the casual clothes. She tried to school her features to an offhand friendliness as her sister answered.

"I am!" Angela laughed in genuine delight. "Toni's out of practice! Set point, Toni!" She lifted her arm to serve.

The volley lasted for several minutes, but finally Toni hit a return out-of-bounds and the game was over. "Whew," she said, "I'm not playing with you again until I've had some practice!" She walked over to the post and picked up her towel to mop her face. "Confess, Angela. You've been taking lessons."

"Well, Jack has helped me some," Angela conceded, giving credit to the boy who had grown up next door.

"Yipes! Didn't Jack play on the university tennis team when he was there?" Jack Blanton was the son of their closest neighbors. He was several years older than Angela, but the three of them had always been good friends.

"Yes, I believe so," Angela admitted innocently.

"And he's been teaching you? I'm impressed." Toni grinned. "What wiles did you use? When we were growing up he never liked to play with girls."

A blush spread over Angela's face. "I guess he just saw what a bad player I was and took pity on me." She tugged at the towel and Toni relinquished it. Angela wiped the perspiration from her own brow.

The good-natured bantering had helped Toni to get over her discomfort at Nick's appearance, and she managed to greet him nonchalantly when he approached.

"I've come to take you girls to lunch."

"Wonderful!" Angela enthused. "Just give us time to change." She slipped her racket into its vinyl cover and zipped it closed.

Toni hesitated. "Not me, thanks. I promised dad I'd visit Uncle Paul today."

The girls' great-uncle was in his nineties and too infirm to leave his home, so he had missed the party the previous evening.

"Oh, Toni, you can visit this afternoon. I'll go with you, but come with us now."

Nick's expression was hidden by dark glasses, but he seconded Angela's urging. "I'll have you back by two o'clock." The three of them walked slowly up the slope of the lawn toward the house.

"Come on, Toni. Nick doesn't take many Saturdays off. You should be honored!"

"All right. I'd like to come, if I won't be a third wheel."

Angela laughed, "Don't be silly!"

Later, under the shower, Toni thought again about Nervy's words last night. She was right. There were no banked fires, no kisses of greeting, no touching. Angela and Nick acted like good friends, not lovers. But perhaps that was as good a basis for marriage as passion. Of course, Nick was a strong self-possessed man. Maybe the fires were there and he kept them well hidden. Toni thought about her own mother. When she died the light seemed to go out in her father. What would it be like to love someone so desperately that there wasn't room for anyone else?

Toni was twisting her hair into its usual smooth coil when Angela knocked. "Are you ready?" she called.

"Almost. Come in."

Angela entered in a cloud of L'air du Temps and a soft pink silk shirtwaist dress. She frowned at Toni's tailored navy blue pantsuit with its crisp white blouse. "Honestly, Toni! Why do you insist on wearing dark colors all the time? They don't do a thing for you."

"Thanks a lot!"

Remorsefully Angela came over to give her sister a hug. "You know I don't mean to be catty. But I do get impatient! You're a beautiful girl, and you seem to do everything you can to hide it."

"I don't!"

"You do! Maybe you don't mean to, but you do. It seems I'm going to have to take you in hand, little sister." Angela faced her, hands on her hips. "Now, take your hair down."

"No!" Toni raised her hands to the coil defensively, but Angela wouldn't yield. Ruthlessly she pulled the pins out, and when the tawny tresses fell below Toni's shoulders she picked up the hairbrush.

"There! Isn't that better?" she asked a few minutes later, standing back to survey her work.

Toni sighed as she looked in the mirror. "Yes, but it will get in my way."

"When your nose is buried in a book, maybe, but not when you're having lunch with a handsome man!"

An hour later Toni watched the engaged couple over the rim of her wineglass. They certainly were a striking pair. Angela's pale blond hair curled softly around the heart-shaped face. When her blue eyes met the brown ones of her fiancé, the expression of gentle sweetness was no different from the gaze she bestowed on any of her friends.

And Nick looked back at her with tender affection, but there was no hunger in his gaze.

Toni frowned at herself in annoyance. Who was she to judge? She had never been in love, but she knew that she wanted more from it than Angela and Nick had.

The waiter served their lunch, and Toni abandoned her observation to concentrate on the luscious salad in front of her. She had not been to this restaurant before. The Hamlet was one of many casual eating places springing up all over Atlanta. The Victorian decor was beautiful. Polished brass and deep-toned mahoghany vied with panes of delicately etched glass. Above their heads were a number of old-fashioned ceiling fans, and the easy movement of air ruffled the broad-leafed palms set here and there in large pots.

Nick had ordered one of the exotic hamburgers for

which the spot was famous, but Toni and Angela both chose the spinach salad.

Suddenly Toni felt two heavy hands on her shoulders. She leaned her head back to see who it was and was soundly kissed. "Jack!"

When Jack hugged her enthusiastically she glanced over to catch a disapproving frown on Nick's face. Did the two men not get along? That was odd. Jack had always been a most amiable fellow. Lifting her arms around his neck, she returned the hug. She was breathless; whether from the hard embrace or from Nick's black scowl, she wasn't sure. "How wonderful to see you!" she exclaimed. "Where were you last night?"

Nick had risen to his feet. "Won't you join us, Blanton?" he invited, and Jack took the seat that was offered.

"Hello, Angela," he said quietly.

"Hi, Jack," she answered, her voice soft.

Toni looked at them blankly. They seemed to be avoiding each other's eyes. What was going on here? They had always been such good friends. Then Jack answered her question and she forgot the incident.

"I had to take the folks to the plane. They're off on another trip." He sighed with a rueful grin.

Toni leaned over to pat his hand. "Do they still travel as much as they used to?"

Jack nodded. "Even more, now that I'm able to run the business while dad's away. It keeps me busy."

"You're not too busy to teach my sister to beat me at tennis!" Toni teased.

There was a heavy silence. Jack threw a fleeting glance at Angela. His fair skin reddened. Then he recovered himself. "So she beat you, did she?" He laughed, but the humor was forced.

"Solidly!" Toni admitted. "I wish you could teach me to serve like that."

"You're on! This summer when you get home."

"I won't have much time. I'm going to take a vacation before I start to look for a job." Toni started to explain about her plans, but she glanced over at Nick and caught a look of annoyance on his face, so she asked instead, "Tell me about the trip your parents are taking, Jack."

The Blantons had always traveled a lot, leaving a younger Jack in the care of a sour-faced butler. Whenever his parents were away, Nervy always made sure the child next door was included in any plans for Angela and Toni. She had him over at the slightest excuse, and the lonely boy loved her at least as much as her own charges did. Their home had become a second home for Jack. She and Angela took turns having tremendous crushes on him. Tall and blond with laughing blue eyes, he had matured easily from football hero to eligible bachelor.

He glanced at his watch. "Oh, they're in Amsterdam by now. And how is our 'almost' lady lawyer doing?" Jack's arm rested along the back of her chair. "You look fantastic." He grinned.

Toni shifted uncomfortably in her chair under his sweeping assessment. "I'm fine," she answered. "Almost fine, anyway. I'll be even better two months from now."

"Did my uncle's firm in Baltimore get in touch with you?" asked Jack.

"Yes, they did," Toni answered enthusiastically. "I went down from Boston to talk to them. Your uncle was very kind. He offered me a job, but I'm not sure...." Her voice trailed off.

"Somehow I always thought you'd come back home." Jack was a sentimentalist about Atlanta.

She smiled fondly at him. "Well, as a matter of fact, I had an offer of a job here just last night." Her gaze swung to Nick.

He and Angela had remained silent, but now his eyes caught and held hers. "It's still open," he said studiedly.

"That would be wonderful, Toni," Angela put in. "I'd love to have you close."

Toni broke Nick's gaze and looked at her sister. "Thank you, Angela, but I doubt that I'll end up in Atlanta."

"I don't blame you for turning that one down," Jack said, his tone suddenly harsh. "It couldn't be too comfortable working for your brother-in-law."

An uncomfortable silence descended immediately like a thick blanket. Toni looked from Jack to Nick, questioning. The hostility between the two men was almost tangible, and Angela's head was bowed, her face flushed. An answer occurred to her. Nick must be jealous of Jack. He probably didn't understand the brother-sister relationship they enjoyed. But Jack? He had always been so easygoing and agreeable.

TONI WAS TO REMEMBER THAT THOUGHT after dinner that evening. Jack and Nick had joined their family group at home, and Jack seemed definitely put out about something.

Even Agnes noticed. "Jack, you're very quiet tonight," she said, handing him his coffee. They had moved to the living room after dinner.

He seemed to recall where he was and visibly forced himself to be charming. "Sorry, Agnes. I was trying to decide the best way to coerce your younger daughter into an intimate little tête-à-tête on the terrace."

Toni's mouth dropped open, but Agnes laughed. "Well, why don't you just ask her?" she encouraged.

"That's an idea. Miss Antonia, will you take the air with me?" He bowed formally and put down the coffee cup.

Toni laughed lightly at the old-fashioned turn of phrase and laid her hand gracefully on the outstretched arm. "Why, Mistuh Blanton, Ah'd be delighted," she said, playing her Southern accent to the limit.

Angela's laugh sounded hollow to Toni's ears. "Nick, now you see a true Southern gentleman in his element."

Nick met Toni's eyes. His expression was unreadable. "Really? Maybe I should take lessons."

There was an undercurrent to this situation that Toni didn't understand. The tension was stretched to a breaking point. That much was obvious, but why? Jack led her through the French doors out into the night. They wandered along the edge of the terrace until they could no longer hear the conversation from inside.

"Would you like to tell me what this is all about?" Toni asked him.

He answered with a question. "You're looking especially delectable tonight. Why shouldn't I want to get you alone?"

"That wasn't what I meant and you know it! Why do you and Nick dislike each other so much?" she demanded.

Jack didn't answer. Hands at her waist, he lifted her to sit on the wall. Their eyes were on the same level. His hands lingered, and his eyes roved over her face suggestively.

Toni tried to wriggle free of his grasp. "Jack, stop it! What are you up to?"

"I like that dress." He ignored her question. "You're really beautiful, Toni."

Angela had insisted on lending her a dress from her own extensive wardrobe. The pale peach color was flattering on her she knew, but the slash of the neckline was revealing, and she was uncomfortable with it. Now Jack's hands were on her back, urging her gently closer to him. "It's Angela's dress," she told him.

His hands dropped immediately as though they had been burned, and he thrust them into the pockets of his white dinner jacket.

"What do you think of Superman, in there?" His head indicated the door.

Toni looked at him in amazement. She had never

heard that note of sarcasm in his voice. "What do you mean?" she asked.

"Mr. Everything-to-everybody."

Toni laughed nervously. "Why, Jack! You almost sound jealous."

There was a fleeting look of bleakness on his face before he turned away. "Don't be ridiculous."

Her eyes widened. So that was it! Jack was in love with Angela, and Nick must have realized it. She stretched out a hand to turn him back to face her. "I'm sorry," she said gently. "Does she know?"

"No! And I'll throttle you if you say one word," he bit out.

Toni was relieved to be back on their old footing. "Don't be silly! I'm not going to say anything. You ought to know that, Jack."

He ran an impatient hand through his hair. "I do know it." His shoulders slumped. "She's not in love with him, Toni. I know she isn't!" Toni's heart did a crazy little skip. "She got herself engaged just to get Agnes off her back!"

"Maybe...." Toni hesitated. "But she'll have to find it out for herself, Jack," she said gently. "We can't interfere."

He gave a long deep sigh. "I know. I'm sorry I snapped at you. Good old Toni. Completely reliable," he chuckled.

Toni wasn't sure she liked his compliment. "Why didn't you ever let Angela know how you felt? You must know that we've both always been half in love with you."

"I just waited too long. Or didn't wake up in time," he said heavily. Then he looked at Toni, speculation growing again in his blue eyes. "Both of you? Maybe if I can't have one sister, I should try for the other."

A spark of anger pricked her. "That isn't very flattering!" She jumped down from her perch and started toward the door.

Jack caught her arm. "I'm sorry, Toni. You're right. It was thoughtless. It's just that this has been a hell of a week for me."

Toni forgave him quickly. "That's okay, Jack. I know how you feel."

"You do?" He raised an eyebrow.

"Well, I mean, I can imagine." She avoided looking at him.

Jack rested against the wall, watching her contemplatively, but instead of pursuing it he switched the subject. "Have you noticed that Nervy doesn't look well?" he asked.

A worried frown creased her brow. "Yes," she answered. "I asked her about it and she said she was just tired. I intend to talk to Douglas. Is there more to it than that, Jack?"

"I don't know." He hesitated. "You know she would never complain to us. I do know that Nick convinced her to check into Emory University Hospital for a checkup. They kept her for three days. She just got home yesterday."

"Yesterday! Why didn't she tell me?" Toni was hurt.

"I'm sure she didn't want to worry you, Toni. And if it were something really serious she would have told us, wouldn't she?"

Toni recognized his need for reassurance. Nervy meant as much to him as she did to her and Angela. "I'm sure she would have. I'll go in to see her before I go to bed."

"You know, Toni, I'm worried about her."

Sympathy softened her gaze. "I understand, Jack." She lifted herself on tiptoe to kiss his cheek.

His arm came around to steady her just as Nick and Angela came through the French doors. Suddenly his embrace tightened. He turned his head and his mouth covered hers firmly.

Toni pushed at his shoulder and he immediately released her. She started to say something sharp, but one look at the pain in his eyes and she closed her mouth. If the kiss camouflaged his feelings, maybe it could work that way for her, too. She relaxed and laid her head against his shoulder.

Both Nick and Angela frowned at the sight that greeted them, but Angela recovered first. "I hope we're not interrupting anything profound."

"Of course not," Toni answered evenly. "If you all will excuse me, I'm having an early night. My flight leaves at 6:45 in the morning."

"Toni! Why so early?" Angela asked.

"It was the only nonstop flight I could get," Toni lied. The sooner she could get back to Boston the better off she would be. "Good night."

She went quietly down the hall near the kitchen.

When she knocked on the door to Nervy's apartment it was opened almost immediately by Douglas.

"Come in, Toni." He stepped back for her to enter. "Minerva has gone to bed, but somehow I thought you might come." He smiled, but his long face held no humor.

"Douglas, what's wrong with her? She told me she was just tired, but tonight Jack said she'd been in Emory Hospital for tests." She laid a hand on his arm. "Is it serious?"

"Let's sit down," he said.

Toni settled into a rocking chair, Nervy's chair, on one side of the small fireplace, and Douglas sat in his easy chair opposite her. Toni looked around her at the cluttered but comfortable room. She had always loved it. She remembered with nostalgia how many times as a child she had crept in here for comfort and reassurance.

"Minerva will have my scalp probably, but since you already know about the hospital...." He leaned forward, elbows on his knees, and dropped his head. "Some of the test results will take a few weeks. The doctors believe that she has a glandular disorder. So far they haven't been able to pinpoint what's wrong." He lifted his head. "We've been married for forty-five years," he said sorrowfully. "This is the first time I've ever known anything to get Minerva down. I don't know what I would do if anything happened to her," he choked.

Toni rose and put a comforting hand on his shoulder. "Douglas, I'm sure the doctors will find the problem and make it right." Her heart was troubled, but she forced herself to be cheerful. "Now, don't you go around with a long face. That would just make her feel worse. She adores you."

"Humph!" The old man straightened and got to his feet. "Bullies me and orders me around! But I sure would miss it if—"

"Douglas! Don't talk like that!" Toni admonished sternly, but she, too, was desolate at the thought. "My plane leaves early tomorrow so I'd better go up to bed. Please call me, Douglas, as soon as you know something."

"I'll try."

"Don't worry. I'll call you." Toni was startled by the deep voice from the doorway.

"Nick!"

"She's in bed, Douglas?"

"Yes, Mr. Trabert. She seemed to be more tired than usual tonight." He slumped in his chair and brushed a hand across his eyes.

Nick clapped a reassuring hand on his shoulder. "You look as if you could use a good night's sleep, too, Douglas. We'll leave you now. Call me if you need anything."

"Thank you, Mr. Trabert. I appreciate everything you've done."

"Good night, Douglas," Toni said as Nick guided her through the door.

"Good night, Toni."

When the door was closed behind them, Toni turned to Nick. "You've been very good. Nervy means a lot to all of us." Her eyes glowed with quiet gratitude. "Thank you," she said sincerely.

Nick's arm circled her shoulder. The warmth of his hand on her bare skin was stirring urgent feelings again. Toni wanted nothing so much as to lay her head against the broad chest. She knew she should pull away, but for now all her self-possession and resolve seemed to have evaporated. They walked back down the hallway.

"I like Nervy," Nick said.

Toni dropped her head. "She likes you, too. I just can't understand why daddy and Agnes didn't realize something was wrong. Jack said you were the one who insisted she go to the hospital."

His arm tightened spasmodically for a moment, then he dropped it. "I don't see her every day. Perhaps that's why I noticed it before they did."

They had reached the stairway. Toni took one step up and turned to face him. "You will call me if you learn something?"

He nodded absently and then, as though he had to touch her, he slipped a hand under the heavy hair at her nape, for a moment looking deep into her eyes. He seemed to be searching for something. "Your sister is a wonderful woman," he murmured.

Toni stiffened at the reminder. "Yes. She is," she answered dismally. "I love her very much. I would never do anything to hurt her." She was trying to warn him, but it came out more as a lament. This awareness between them—neither could deny it and neither tried—was dangerous.

"I'd never hurt her, either. I hope you believe that," Nick said huskily.

"Of course."

Suddenly Nick tore his eyes from her gaze. He rammed his fists into his pockets and turned to reenter the living room. "I'll call you. Good night, Toni," he said over his shoulder.

"Good night," she said to his stiff back. She stood looking after him for a moment. It was a good thing she was leaving. The more she saw of this man the more she realized... realized what?

As she climbed the stairs she admitted to herself that she was running. Whether away from Nick and Angela or toward the peaceful sanctuary of her apartment in Boston, she didn't know. But she was definitely running.

The moonlight was enough illumination as she undressed. Her thoughts were in a turmoil. She slipped into a creamy lace teddy and was turning back the covers of the bed when she heard the front door close.

Despite herself, she was drawn to the open window that overlooked the driveway.

Nick's long legs were taking him with a certain reluctance to his car. His hands were thrust into the pockets of his trousers, his black jacket unbuttoned. The moonlight turned his white shirtfront to silver, making his chest look unbelievably broad.

Just as he reached the car and put out a hand to the door he paused and lifted his eyes to her window. He must have felt her gaze; he couldn't possibly know which room was hers, but the force of his eyes was like an electrical current. She couldn't read the expression on his face—they were too far apart for that—but she knew that the strange hunger she felt was mirrored there. She took a nervous step back, out of the path of the moonlight.

He stood frozen, staring for a long minute, and then she could feel the power of his will as he withdrew from the almost mystical threads of awareness between them. He got into the car and slammed the door with much more force than was necessary.

Toni stared blankly after the retreating lights of his car. Then she sank onto the padded window seat and buried her face in her arms on the sill. Oh, God! This was awful. Her emotions had taken a battering and she couldn't wait to get away to safety. She was tired, overworked and under a tremendous amount of pressure. That was why she was reacting this way. That had to be why. She sat like that for a long time, letting the softness of the spring night caress her shoulders, heal her with its warm breeze, its sweet scent, its sighing soothing sounds.

Gradually she became aware that there were human whispers mingling with the murmur of the breeze. She lifted her head to see two shadowy figures seated side by side on the steps below.

Jack was leaning forward, his hands dangling between his knees, and Angela was turned slightly toward him, her dress billowing gracefully around her. She used her slender hands to punctuate what she was saying.

Toni couldn't hear the whispered words, but she smiled at the gestures. Angela was obviously delivering a lecture.

Suddenly Jack surged to his feet, ramming his hands into the pockets of his dinner jacket. "Dammit, Angela! Don't preach to me!"

"Well, somebody certainly needs to! You're acting like a boor, Jack," Angela accused. "Your manners are appalling."

Jack glared down at her in helpless desperation, and then his hands came out to grasp her shoulders, pulling her up into his arms. His hand held her head immobile, and his mouth covered hers in a passionate kiss. Angela seemed stunned into immobility for a moment, but then she struggled free. "Jack! How could you do such a thing?" she cried fiercely. "I'm engaged!"

"I know, Angel. I know," he said in a low, very sad voice. He turned and strode across the lawn toward the dark house next door.

Angela stood quite still watching him leave. Her hands hugged her arms, warming them against a sudden chill that, as far as Toni could tell, was nonexistent.

Just before he reached the gap in the hedge Jack turned back. "Give Toni a message for me. Tell her that I'll pick her up at five o'clock to take her to the airport." In the quiet night air his voice carried clearly, though the words were spoken in the same low voice.

Toni's brows lifted at that.

Angela nodded in an abstracted way. "I'll tell her." Her voice was oddly husky.

"Do you want to ride along?"

"No!" The word was choked out. Angela turned and fled into the house.

Suddenly Toni realized with a flash of guilt that she had been listening to a private conversation. As soon as she heard the front door close on Angela, she carefully slid the window down and scooted across the room to jump into bed. She pulled the covers up to her ears and closed her eyes.

Light from the hallway spilled in her face a few minutes later. She blinked and sat up, yawning. The light was behind Angela and she couldn't see her expression, but she could feel her sister's agitation. "Hi, Angela. Did you want to talk?" she asked gently.

Angela came farther into the room. "No, you're tired." She smiled, but there was a trace of confusion in her voice. "Jack said to tell you that he would drive you to the airport tomorrow. He'll pick you up at five."

Toni put surprise into her voice and eyes. "Oh, really? That's nice of him." She reached out to turn on the bedside lamp. The sudden illumination startled Angela. Toni wasn't surprised to see the becoming flush on her cheeks.

Angela hesitated. "Well, good night, Toni. Thanks again for coming." She seemed to want to say more.

"Are you sure you don't want to stay for a while?"

"I don't think so." She came over to give Toni a warm hug and murmured good night.

When she had left Toni sat for a long time, clasping her knees to her chest and thinking.

THE TRIP TO THE AIRPORT was accomplished much quicker in the early-morning hours. Toni was privately dreading what was to come. Jack loved her like a sister but getting up at this time of day was a rare event for him. Yet there was a purpose to his thoughtfulness, and she was afraid she knew what it was. Sure enough, they were only halfway there when he brought up the matter that was weighing heavily on his mind.

"Toni, I need to talk to you."

"Do you have to?" she groaned, but she grinned at him.

"So, you've figured it out, have you?" He answered her smile with one that lightened his expression considerably.

"It wasn't too difficult. You are not known to be an early riser, my friend."

Suddenly he sobered. "I haven't been to bed," he said calmly.

Toni sat up straight. Was there a new confidence to the bearing of his shoulders, a strong determination in his voice? Jack had always been a happy-go-lucky fellow, never quite serious. Surely his chin hadn't always been set in such a stubborn angle.

"I stayed awake all night trying to reach a decision about Angela, and I've decided to tell her, Toni." He pushed his chin out farther. "I'm going to tell her how I feel," he declared.

I'm sure she has an inkling after that kiss, thought Toni, but she didn't make the comment out loud.

"She should have a choice," he continued.

"Well...." Toni didn't know what to say, especially in light of her own reaction to Nick Trabert.

Jack hit the steering wheel with a fist. "Dammit, Toni!" he erupted. "I love her! I can't just let her go without a fight!" The anguish was there, and the pain; and they were deep.

Toni's heart went out to this dear friend of many years. "Then you *should* tell her. Let her make the decision." She took a long breath and added, "But you must abide by her choice, Jack."

His shoulders slumped. "I know, and that will be the hardest part. She thinks of me as a brother. But dammit, I don't feel like her brother!" He glanced across and suddenly grinned. "She is beautiful, isn't she?"

Toni smiled indulgently. "Yes, Jack, she is beautiful, and sweet, and honest, and loving." She ticked off each characteristic on her fingers. Then her hand dropped. "And if you do anything to hurt her I'll bash you over the head!"

His voice was very soft and tender. "I would never hurt her...I love her too much."

Toni swallowed past the lump in her throat.

"But I intend to put up a hell of a fight for her," he finished resolutely.

When the plane was airborne, Toni relaxed in her

seat and thought back over the conversation. Poor Jack. He was a dear, but how could he ever compete with the dynamic appeal of a man like Nick Trabert? She shook her head sadly and reached for a magazine.

4

MONDAY AFTERNOON Professor Winter announced in class that they would have a guest lecturer one week from Friday.

"He is Nicholas Trabert, one of our former students, who has become an authority on contracts. He has been practicing law in Atlanta for the past twelve years. He travels extensively to speak on the subject, and I felt that you should have the opportunity to hear him before you begin to prepare for your final examinations." He looked directly at Toni. Professor Winter, ever dignified in the navy blue suits he always wore, had a round face and thatch of white hair faintly reminiscent of Santa Claus. But there the likeness ended. He never let anything as frivolous as a smile cross his serious demeanor, but Toni thought she caught a gleam of something—recognition?—in his eyes as he looked at her. He went on to describe Nick's credentials and accomplishments in the field, and Toni realized that she had been correct in her assessment that Nick was an expert.

Still, as the days flew by, Toni wished more and more often that he weren't coming. Since her trip to

Atlanta, her sister's fiancé intruded into her thoughts with uncomfortable regularity. She remembered the touch of his hand on her back when they were dancing, the warmth of his smile, the tangy elusive smell of his after-shave. He hadn't called her yet to report on Nervy's condition, but as the two weeks became one and the days dwindled, a nervous excitement grew inside her at the prospect of seeing him. She struggled with herself, but the feeling was impossible to repress. Nick's strong features would appear before her at the most inconvenient times.

Like a giant inside of her, swelling her heart, the burden of guilt mounted in proportion to the anticipation. She refused to rationalize her feelings by telling herself that Angela wasn't really in love with Nick. That was a coward's way out. Angela wore his ring and that made her his. She herself had no right to dwell on memories and dreams of a man who belonged to another.

Angela wasn't very good at correspondence, but Toni received one letter from her. It was full of news about the country-club set, mutual friends and her tennis game. Only once at the end, did she mention her fiancé. "Nick is looking forward to taking you to dinner while he's in Boston," she wrote. "Y'all have fun!"

The sweet trust in the phrase brought a surge of remorse to Toni. After all, this was simply a strong physical attraction she felt. She certainly was not in love with the man, was she?

Mentally she shook herself and refused to think

further about such an idea. Obviously that path led to disaster. Look at Jack. She remembered the scene she had witnessed on the night before her return to Boston, remembered the dejection in the slump of Jack's shoulders as he walked across the lawn in the moonlight. If she ever found herself in love with Nick...no! It couldn't even be considered.

When Toni left the campus each afternoon to return to her apartment to study, she found her feet taking her the two blocks to the Public Gardens where she lingered for an hour or so. The trees had begun to bud, and row upon row of bright red tulips stood tall. Spring sunshine sparkled on the lake. Toni often wandered through the park to the water's edge, standing for long minutes watching the swans' graceful movements. Everywhere she looked people and animals seemed to be in pairs. There was an elderly couple who sat on the same bench each day feeding the squirrels. The beautiful weather had brought out the lovers and all around, everyone belonged to someone, except her.

Toni recognized her affliction as spring fever, but she couldn't seem to discover a remedy, or lose herself in her books the way she'd always been able to do.

One day, toward the middle of the second week, she returned to her apartment in a particularly pensive mood. The phone was ringing, and she dropped her books on the sofa as she crossed to answer it. "Hello," she said listlessly.

"Toni? This is Nick."

The identification was unnecessary. The minute he spoke her name her heart gave a great lurch in her chest. She gripped the receiver tightly and struggled to speak past the frozen lump in her throat. "Hi, Nick," she managed.

"How are you?" His deep voice sent chills over her.

"I'm fine." Fine! She was shaking like a new leaf in the spring breeze. She took a deep steadying breath. "How's Nervy?" she asked.

"She's not a great deal better." The caressing tone changed to a businesslike one, which helped Toni to get a grip on herself. "Her doctor wants her to come to the Boston Medical Center. It seems he trained under a specialist there and would like his old teacher to examine her."

"When is she coming?" Knowing Nervy's aversion to travel, Toni was worried.

"The doctor is out of town until a week from Saturday." He chuckled. "I just hope I can bully her into coming by then."

"I'll call her. She has to come, Nick! We just couldn't get along without her." She took a breath. "None of us could."

There was a long pause. "She's like a mother to you, isn't she?"

"Yes," she said softly. "Even more. Nervy was always there when we needed her."

"Don't worry, Toni. We'll get her to Boston if I have to carry her on the plane myself." There was a hint of steel in his voice, and Toni was sure he would do just that.

"Thank you, Nick."

He hesitated. "It's good to hear your voice, Toni," he said easily.

What could she answer to that? It was good to hear his voice, too. It was heaven. It ignited little tongues of flame in her midsection. And...and he belonged to her sister, she told herself firmly. "How...how is Angela?"

"Angela's fine," he answered shortly. "Still taking tennis lessons!"

"Oh." He sounded put out. Was he jealous of Jack? She wanted to reassure him, but before she could speak he gave a harsh laugh.

"I'll see you in a couple of days, Toni."

"Oh...yes. Thank you for calling."

"Goodbye...Toni. See you soon," he said drawing the words out as though he hated to break the contact.

Toni replaced the receiver slowly.

TONI'S STUDY GROUP was now meeting nightly during the week, reviewing the year's work in preparation for finals. A group of eight students had gathered during the first year of law school to study together before exams. There were only six of them left, and as graduation neared they seemed to draw closer. They had known each other so well for three years, but in less than two months they would scatter. They all were saddened by the prospect.

There was only one other woman in the group besides Toni: Mary Ann Kendall, and she was married. There was that pairing again!

The group had gathered at Toni's apartment on the night before Nick was to arrive. Toni had to fight to concentrate on the discussion. Nick's face kept appearing on the pages of her notes. If she hadn't thought Professor Winter would use on their final exam, some of the lecture material Nick would be presenting, she would have arranged to be sick! But she didn't dare miss the class.

"Toni?"

She glanced up to find her friends all looking at her. "I'm sorry. What?"

The unelected leader of the group, Steven Stonehill, grinned. "Come back to us," he teased.

Toni gave a rueful smile. "I don't know what's wrong with me," she sighed.

Steven looked around at the group and then proclaimed, "Well, I do! It's what's wrong with each one of us—all work and no play! I'm calling a meeting tomorrow night at Fridays. And here are my instructions." He stood and began to pick up his books and notes. Everyone else followed suit with a sense of relief. "You may bring a date or your spouse." He bowed to Mary Ann. "But under penalty of expulsion do not bring a thought of a brief, a tort or a contract!"

They all laughed. Fridays was a Boston night spot, popular with students. "What a wonderful idea! Maybe it's just the therapy we need! Hallelujah!"

they said, moving toward the door. "See you tomorrow night!"

When they had all left except Steven, he asked Toni, "Can I pick you up or will you want to bring someone?"

Toni thought fleetingly of the dinner invitation Nick had given her in Atlanta. Even though she hadn't accepted, it would seem strange if she didn't see him at all while he was in town, unless she had a good excuse. Relieved at this unexpected reason to refuse Nick, she said gaily, "Thanks, Stephen. I won't be bringing anyone."

"I'll come by about eight then. Bye, Toni."

When she closed the door after him she leaned against it in relief. If Nick was coming to Boston on business he would be leaving on Saturday. No one did business on Sunday. And now she had a plausible excuse for Friday night.

Toni undressed and climbed into bed. She fell into a deep sleep almost immediately. It was the first unbroken night's sleep she'd had in two weeks.

THE NEXT AFTERNOON Toni walked into class feeling relaxed. The rest had done her good. She had wakened in the morning feeling more able to cope with seeing Nick again. It was an unhappy situation but one she would have to deal with alone. Nick knew the effect he had on her. When he and Angela were married—the thought sent a shiver down her spine—she would just have to avoid visits and family gatherings. She loved Angela deeply and already felt that she had betrayed her. Now she resolved not to let what was simply a physical attraction become anything more.

She put her books down on the desk next to Mary Ann's and shrugged out of her blue sweater. Her neat plaid blouse and navy blue slacks fit well over her curves. She had braided her hair into a single pigtail, which hung down her back.

Mary Ann leaned over to ask, "Are you going to Fridays tonight?"

Toni folded her sweater across the back of her seat. "Yes, Steven's picking me up. Are you and Joe coming?"

Mary Ann made a face. "We can't. Joe's parents called this morning. They're coming into town for the weekend, so we're going to dinner with them."

Mary Ann's husband was a student at Massachusetts Institute of Technology. His parents often came into the city from their home up the coast in Maine. Mary Ann called the trips their "periodical inspections" to make sure she was caring well for their only son.

Toni sympathized. "Maybe you can join us later. If I know our crew, we'll be there till the wee hours." She sat down.

"We'll try to. My God! Who is that?" Mary Ann's head had swiveled around and Toni followed her gaze. She almost laughed out loud at Mary Ann's reaction, but her own heart began to pound uncomfortably.

Professor Winter had entered the room through the door from his office, and Nick was with him.

Toni whispered, "That's our lecturer for today—Nick Trabert."

Nick's eyes found her immediately. They warmed as they skimmed over her and he smiled.

"You know him?" Mary Ann was impressed.

"Yes. He's—" At a glare from Professor Winter she broke off.

The professor introduced Nick briefly and sat down in a chair to one side.

When Nick walked to the podium Toni's mouth suddenly became very dry. He was dressed in a charcoal-gray suit that molded the broad shoulders to perfection. His white shirt made his tanned face seem even darker, and when he smiled the flash of white even teeth aroused an ache deep in Toni's body. She moistened her lips with the tip of her tongue and swallowed.

Nick's observant eyes didn't miss the action. He lifted a brow and Toni tried to look composed. His mouth quirked before he looked around the room. Strangely there was no need for verbal communication between them. He began to speak, and at the sound of that low impelling voice, Toni's power of reason flew out the open window into the warm spring air. She hoped desperately that someone in her study group was taking notes, because she couldn't tear her eyes away from that powerful male figure.

Moving easily, Nick's talk flowed. He didn't meet Toni's eyes. In fact he seemed to be looking everywhere in the room but at her. At one point he unbuttoned the coat of his suit and shoved his hands into his trouser pockets, tightening them over the muscular thighs. He was vigorous and forceful and unbelievably handsome.

When the lecture concluded, hearty applause broke out spontaneously from the class. He grinned, thanking them, and asked for questions. A dozen hands shot up. Nick fielded the questions skillfully, and at the end of the hour Professor Winter had to call a halt. He dismissed the class adding, "Miss Grey, would you remain, please?"

She received some curious looks as she gathered up her books and sweater and went slowly down the steps to the front of the quickly emptying classroom.

Professor Winter shook hands with Nick. She could hear him as he said his warm goodbyes and thanks.

"Thank you, sir. I'm honored that you asked me to speak." He watched the professor leave the room before he turned to observe her reluctant approach. His arms were rigid, and where he gripped each side of the podium, his knuckles were white. "Hello, Toni," he said quietly.

"Hello, Nick." It seemed like a year instead of only two weeks since she had been this close to him. Her heart pounded irregularly while she struggled desperately to appear casual. "It's good to see you." Her eyes were captured in the darkness of his.

He laughed under his breath. "It's good to see you, too. Will you give me a ride?" he asked with an easy grin.

"A ride? Where are you staying?"

"I have an aunt who lives in Boston. I'm staying with her." He paused, then asked formally, "Will you have dinner with me?"

Toni took a deep breath and tore her eyes away. "Yes, I'll give you a ride, but no, I can't have dinner. I have a date."

Toni hadn't noticed that Steven had followed her until she felt a hand on her shoulder. She turned to look up at him and missed Nick's quick frown.

"I'll pick you up at eight," he reminded and looked at Nick expectantly.

Toni nodded and, when the younger man still didn't leave, succumbed to the inevitable. "Nick Trabert, this is Steven Stonehill."

"Mr. Trabert, I'm really glad to meet you. Your lecture was great!" They shook hands.

"Call me Nick, Steven. I'm glad you enjoyed it." He turned to Toni. "I'm really sorry you have a date tonight, Toni. What about—"

Toni closed her eyes and almost groaned aloud as Steven picked up on it and interrupted, "Why, it's not really a date! Our study group is just getting together at Fridays. We'd be honored to have you join us, Nick."

Nick's fathomless black eyes were on her as she opened her blue ones and looked at him cautiously.

"I might just do that, Steven," he said, releasing her gaze.

"Good! We'll see you there." Steven looked from one of them to the other. "Do you still want me to pick you up, Toni?"

"Yes, please," she murmured. Her head was bent, and her fingers nervously plucked at a corner of paper in her notebook.

"Okay. Eight o'clock." Steven left.

There was a long silence in the empty room before Nick said in a husky voice, "Are you going to give me a ride, Toni?"

She kept her head down but nodded. After a two-week separation he still exerted that magnetic pull. She wanted so much to throw herself in his arms.

He came closer and lifted her chin with a finger. "Do you know," he mused, "the last time I saw you you were naked."

"Naked!" The word escaped far more loudly than she intended and she looked around. She relaxed when she saw that the room was empty. "I was not!" she hissed at him through her teeth.

"Oh yes. You were." He repeated his assertion with a nonchalance that was maddening.

Toni thought back. At dinner? At her parents' house? Then she remembered the moment at the window. Her face turned a becoming shade of rose. "I had on a teddy," she informed him haughtily.

"A what?" he laughed. "I thought that was something you slept with." The sight of his grin was luscious, but she forced her eyes away from his handsome face.

"That's a teddy *bear*! This is a teddy. It's a... well, it...anyway, I sleep *in* it!"

A dark brow climbed and a muscle in his jaw twitched. "Sounds interesting," he said smoothly.

"This is a ridiculous conversation!" Toni turned to leave the room, but before she could take more than a step or two she was brought up short by a firm hand holding the pigtail that hung down her back.

Her hand went to her head. "Ouch! Nick, let go!" She was juggling her books in one arm, and a heavy volume slid to the floor with a loud smack that sounded like a gunshot.

Nick reached for the book with one hand but still held on to the pigtail with the other. "Not until you tell me what's bothering you." He towered over her, frowning.

Toni looked up. "Please, Nick," she said stiffly. "Just drop it!"

For a moment he studied her face as if unsure whether she meant the subject or her pigtail. He sighed deeply and dropped both. "Let's go," he said impatiently.

"Where does your aunt live?" Toni asked as they climbed into her small red sports car. She had left the top down, as it was such a beautiful day, and she'd tossed her books over the seat into the back.

"Not far from you. You're on CommAve near the gardens, aren't you?" Nick had shortened the name of Commonwealth Avenue the way a native Bostonian did, and Toni looked at him in surprise.

"Are you originally from Boston? I noticed when we met that you didn't have a Southern accent."

"I'm from Quincy, Massachusetts, but, like you, I spent seven years in school in Boston." He grinned. "Seven long years, aren't they?"

She nodded and grinned back, "Very long!" The tenseness between them eased.

"How did you happen to end up in Atlanta?" Toni maneuvered the car into the traffic, glad to have a topic for inconsequential conversation.

"I had an offer from a good firm there when I got out of school." As he talked Nick loosened his discreetly striped blue tie, opened the top button of his shirt and settled back in the bucket seat. "I stayed three years before I decided that what I really wanted to be was my own boss, so I went out alone."

Toni threw him a sideways glance. She could easily imagine this forceful independent man wanting to be his own boss. In fact, she couldn't imagine him any other way.

After they crossed the Charles River, Toni began to edge toward the left lane in anticipation of her turn. "You still haven't said where you're going," she reminded him.

"My aunt lives on Beacon Hill."

"Oh, I've missed the turn!"

"It doesn't matter. I'll walk from your apartment. It's a beautiful day and I need the exercise." He rubbed a tired hand over his face. "I feel as if I've lived in airplanes for the past two weeks." He half turned in his seat, so that he was facing her. He took the opportunity to survey her from head to toe, his expression clearly appreciative.

"And I want to see where you live," he added.

Toni felt his intense regard and her cheeks warmed. She hoped he wouldn't notice her blush, but she should have realized that nothing escaped his observant eyes.

"Do I make you uncomfortable, Toni?" he asked in a level voice.

Her laugh was brittle. "Of course not! Why, you're practically my brother!"

Nick didn't answer for a minute, then he said simply, "Am I?" He raked impatient fingers through his hair. "Toni, I want to explain something to you. Angela and I—"

"Are engaged!" she interrupted sharply. "You may not know how lucky you are, Nick. My sister is a gentle sweet-tempered person."

"Do you think I don't know that?" he grumbled irritably.

Toni eased the small car between two larger ones and turned off the engine with a snap. Deliberately she changed the subject. "It's not often this easy to find a parking place," she said with false gaiety, as she got out of the car. "The average is two circles of the block!"

Nick helped her raise the convertible top and took her books from her while she locked the car. She reached for them but he stopped her, asking with a mocking smile, "Aren't you going to ask me in?"

"I have some studying to do," she said, hedging, "I won't stay long."

Shrugging, she started up the steps. "If you like." She fitted her key into a wrought-iron grilled door.

Following her inside, Nick said, "I really am thirsty. All that talking...."

Toni cocked her head and met his eyes. A teasing light glowed there. For the first time she felt herself unbend in response. "Are you reminding me of my manners?" she asked, beginning to smile.

"I wouldn't dare." He looked down, mischief in his eye, and her heart did a flip.

She laughed and gave in. "Okay. Would you care to come in for something to drink, Mr. Trabert?" she asked with exaggerated politeness.

"That's very hospitable of you, Miss Grey." He bowed her formally into the elevator. "Which floor?" His hand hovered over the panel of buttons.

"Be careful!" Toni warned. "Third floor, but don't touch any of the other buttons at the same time. It throws the poor thing into total confusion! I was stuck in here one time for two hours."

"I'll have to remember that, in case I ever want to get you alone."

Toni didn't answer. Darn him! Why did he have to make remarks like that?

As they entered her apartment she dropped her purse on the sofa and headed toward the tiny kitchen. "Coffee or something cold?" she asked him.

Nick put down her books and followed her into the cubicle. "What do you have?" He leaned across from behind her to peer into the refrigerator.

Toni caught her breath when his shoulder brushed hers. She could smell his after-shave, and even the light contact left her uncertain again.

He must have felt her stiffen because he said nonchalantly, "Coffee sounds good. If I may, I'll have a glass of water first."

Toni reached above her for a glass and opened the top door of the refrigerator, which revealed a small freezer. She dropped ice cubes in the glass and filled it with water from the tap.

As Nick took the glass from her his fingers brushed hers.

Toni's eyes flew to his in shock at the electrical current tingling through her. He put the glass down and with both hands on her shoulders turned her gently to face him. "Toni, don't be frightened of me."

"I'm not," she said bluntly. And that was the truth. She wasn't frightened of him at all. Only of herself and these totally inappropriate feelings she had for her sister's fiancé. "If you'll let go of me, I'll make the coffee."

Nick looked at her for a moment before letting his hands fall away. He picked up the glass and moved into the living room.

With shaking fingers Toni measured water and coffee. When it was perking, she laid out cups on a tray. She went to the door, asking, "Do you take cream and sugar?"

Nick stood with his back to her, looking out through the bay window to the street below. He had discarded his jacket, and his hands were thrust into the pockets of his gray trousers. He didn't turn. "No, just black."

When she reentered the room carrying the tray, Nick took it from her and set it on the coffee table. He picked up his cup and went over to sit in a chair across from the sofa she had settled on. "I like your apartment. How long have you lived here?"

Toni looked around at the gaily patterned chintzes that she had selected with such care, at her mother's secretary, standing tall against one wall. She would have to move soon if she didn't take a job in Boston, and the thought of leaving was at once unhappy and exciting. "Three years. I moved here when I started law school. I really will miss it. It's my first very own home."

"Did you select the artwork, too? It's very good."

Her gaze went to her collection of watercolors, all depicting scenes from the region. In her spare time Toni loved to hunt down obscure art shops. Most of the paintings were of the harbors along the Massachusetts coast and Cape Cod. She nodded, warmed by his praise. "Thank you. There's one there from Quincy. Do you see it?"

Nick pointed to the picture. "Yes. The shipyards. I practically grew up around there. My father was a ship builder." He smiled reminiscently.

"Do your parents still live there?"

"No. My mother died when I was born, and my father two years ago. He never remarried. He always said that she was the one great love of his life." Nick stared into his cup.

Toni caught a moment of unguarded sadness on his face. "I know what you mean." She sighed.

His piercing glance pinned her. "Is Jack Blanton the one great love of your life?" he asked in a bland tone.

She stared at him. His face wore an intense expression, and he sat perfectly still watching her. "Of course not!" She dropped her eyes, then groped for words to further explain. "I...I must not have met mine yet. I meant my father and mother." She took a deep breath. "Nick, I know you're jealous of Jack."

His eyes narrowed. "You do?" he asked in a strange voice.

"But honestly, Jack has been like a brother to Angela and me. If she's seeing a lot of him, it's because they are very good friends."

He laughed unpleasantly. "You're a very naive young lady, Toni, but you're right about one thing: I'm jealous as hell of Blanton." Suddenly he leaned back in his chair and changed the subject. "You must be very like your mother."

"Why do you say that?" She was surprised at the abrupt switch.

"Well, Agnes obviously resents you. She must be jealous." He shrugged as though it were obvious.

Toni was amazed. "That's very perceptive of you," she murmured.

"Not really. Anyone who knows even a little bit about human nature could have figured it out."

"Anyway," Toni said, putting her empty cup on the tray, "now that Angela and I are...are moving into lives of our own, maybe things will be better between daddy and Agnes. I hope so. Daddy and I had a talk before I left."

"I know. He told Angela about it. I was there. You're a very forgiving person to have excused being treated like the proverbial stepchild for so many years. Angela told me how Agnes acts toward you."

Toni rose and began to pace. "Angela shouldn't have said anything. Besides, I always had Nervy." She whirled to face him. "Nervy! Is there anything I should know about Nervy, Nick?"

"Nothing. She told me you telephoned yesterday."

"Yes, and she promised to come next weekend."

Nick got to his feet and replaced his cup on the tray. "Then, that's all. We just have to wait and see." His hand reached out and he stroked her cheek with a knuckle. "It will be all right, Toni."

"I hope so." It was nothing but a reassuring touch, yet she dropped her eyes so that he couldn't see how much she was affected by it.

"I'd better be going. My aunt will be expecting me." He picked up his suit jacket and hooked it over his shoulder. "Will you drive to the Cape with me tomorrow? I have to take care of some business down there for her."

"Tomorrow? But I thought...."

"Thought what?" His eyes narrowed.

"Oh, nothing. I just don't...."

"Come on, Toni," he urged. "Let's get to know each other. You can't go on being afraid of me forever."

"I'm not afraid of you,'" she denied.

"Well...?"

She wanted to be with him. She really wanted to, but her common sense told her it was folly.

Nick took her hesitation for acceptance. "Good! I'll

pick you up about eight. We'll have breakfast with
Aunt Lydia. She'll be disappointed that you couldn't
come for dinner."

"Are you going to be at Fridays?" Toni asked,
dreading his answer.

"I might drop by later. Thanks for the coffee." He
opened the door.

"You're welcome." She moved to close the door
after him, but his hand stopped the motion. His
fingers spread over her cheek and into her hair.
There was a tender illumination in the dark depths
of his eyes, a trace of compassion and something
else—pity? Why would he look at her with pity? Be-
wilderment clouded her eyes for an instant before a
dawning comprehension sent her eyelids down.
Could she love him? She swallowed a small cry as
she faced the horrible fact she'd tried so hard to ignore. She was very probably in love with her sister's
fiancé! How outrageous fate was! Toni Grey, who
had gone blithely through her twenty-four years,
without ever having had more than an occasional
crush, had fallen head over heels for the one man she
could never have. Instinctively she knew this was no
simple physical pull, but a deep enduring emotion.
She opened her eyes again to look at Nick, hoping he
couldn't read what was there.

He studied her for a moment. As he dropped his
arm his fingers brushed her shoulder. "Relax, Toni,"
he said with a smile and was gone.

5

FRIDAYS WAS ON NEWBURY STREET just a few blocks from
Toni's apartment. It was a mild night, so Toni and
Steven decided to walk. Steven locked his car and
playfully pitched her the keys. "If I have too much
beer, put me in a taxi."

"Uh-oh. It sounds like you're planning a wild
night!" Toni admonished. A wry smile deepened the
dimples in her cheeks. She had left her hair down and
wore a pair of faded jeans that fit enticingly over her
well-rounded bottom. A yellow turtleneck sweater
emphasized the uptilted thrust of her breasts, and the
color brought out the blond highlights in her hair.

"Well, this *is* recess!" Steven proclaimed with a
wave of his arm. "And you look fantastically sexy in
that outfit!"

Toni felt a faint sense of dread. Steven was almost
always the most dependable escort. He had made
one or two perfunctory passes when they first met
three years ago, but when Toni had made it clear she
wasn't interested, he seemed relieved. Since that time
they had become very good friends.

Steven had a zeal for a successful career in law,
which blocked out all desire for personal relation-

ships. But periodically he had a night that he called "recess" and, like a child out of school, played until he was played out! Inevitably on those nights he became sentimental and amorous, and Toni shrank from his company.

Fridays was "jumping" that night. As Toni and Steven entered the crowded restaurant-cum-pub, the noise hit them like a brick wall.

Steven leaned down and shouted in her ear, "Stay here!"

Toni nodded and he moved into the crowd, craning his neck to find their friends. In a few minutes he was back and grabbed her hand, pulling her along behind him through the mass of people. When they reached a table in the back the noise was slightly more bearable.

Sam Manley was there alone, guarding a table for six. "This is the best I could do. I'm glad you're here. I don't think I could have held on to it much longer." His freckled face wore an anticipatory grin.

Another member of the group, Peter Godfrey, came in with an attractive brunette whom he introduced simply as Cecily, and a few minutes later, Jim Simpson arrived with his fiancée, Buffy Lovvorn. Buffy was also a law student, one year behind them. As they were settling around the table they discovered they were one chair short, and Steven braved the ire of the people in a group nearby to pull one over.

The waiter finally approached to take their order. Steven asked Toni, "What will you have to drink? We'll eat later."

Toni asked for a glass of white wine, and the cool tangy taste when it came was satisfying. She sat with her back to the wall, content to observe and listen, rather than taking part in the merry party. Instead her thoughts turned to the next day's trip to Cape Cod with Nick. She had already begun to dread a whole day spent in his company. It could be disastrous, considering the new knowledge she had of her feelings. Maybe his aunt would go, too, she speculated. That certainly would make it easier.

Steven interrupted her thoughts. "Your glass is empty," he said. He motioned the waiter over and told the man to bring a carafe.

Toni protested, "No, Steven! I'm the only one who's drinking wine. A carafe's too much!"

Steven put an arm around her and nuzzled her ear. "Let your hair down, Toni. This is recess!"

"I'm not going to try to keep up with you, Steven!" she said reprovingly and lifted the arm from around her shoulder. But before long it was back. The evening wore on, and soon it was obvious to Toni that Steven wasn't going to be as easy to handle as he had been in the past. And everyone seemed to forget that they hadn't eaten.

"Let's order something to eat, Steven. I'm hungry." She tried to dissuade him from the affectionate mutterings, which were becoming embarrassing. Her big eyes behind the owlish lenses pleaded with Sam to distract Steven's attention.

Sam got the message. He started to question Steven

about a cruise they were planning to take after graduation.

Toni picked up her wineglass and took a sip. Her
head had begun to swim. How much of this had she
had, she wondered. Every time she sipped from the
glass Steven would refill it. She put the glass down
abruptly and leaned her head against the wall behind her, closing her eyes. She had to get something
to eat!

Toni felt Steven's warm breath on her ear, nuz-
zling again. He tangled his fingers in her long hair.
She pushed at him. "Quit that!" she ordered. She
opened her eyes and looked directly into Nick's
glowering face. He was standing a few feet behind
Buffy's chair, hands thrust into the pockets of his
khaki pants. His brawny shoulders in the navy blue
V-necked cashmere sweater shrugged aside a young
man who stumbled into him. The collar of the blue
oxford-cloth shirt underneath was unbuttoned. She
could see the erratic throbbing of a pulse in his
throat. He was so masculine! And so angry! Toni
gulped and smiled tentatively.

At that moment Steven saw him. "Nick! You made
it!" He got rather unsteadily to his feet, and his
words were slurred as he introduced Nick to the
others at the table. "Pull up a chair, Nick!"

"I don't think there's one to be had, Steven," Nick
said, looking around at the jam of people.

"Here, you can have mine. I'll swipe one somewhere." Steven moved away on rubbery legs, and
Nick came around the table to sit beside Toni.

She held her breath expecting to be scolded, but he only nodded and said, "Toni."

His eyes were cold as they raked her feminine form in the yellow turtleneck sweater and jeans. He turned away in response to a remark about his lecture from one of the others.

Toni was glad that his attention was distracted. His chilly appraisal had disconcerted her, and now she had a chance to study the strong profile. His black hair had fallen forward over his forehead, and he raked it back with an impatient hand. Her eyes lingered on the masterful curve of that sensual mouth, and she wondered how it would feel to be kissed by him. Someone handed him a mug of beer, and as he lifted it to drink, her eyes followed the movement of his big hand. She closed her eyes again and leaned her head back. Her senses were really spinning now as she imagined his hands on her, touching, caressing. She knew with weakening instinct that they could guide a woman to the heights of excitement.

Toni gave a little groan and opened her eyes, reaching for her wineglass. But it wasn't there. She looked around and met Nick's eyes.

"I think you've had enough, don't you?" he asked inflexibly.

Toni lifted her chin. "Certainly not! I'm perfectly sober," she declared bravely, but she felt so thick-headed! She had definitely had enough, but she wasn't going to admit it to him.

"Are you?"

"Well...." She ducked her head. "Almost. If we could just eat, I'm sure I'd be fine."

"Hell! Do you mean you haven't eaten?"

Toni shook her head. "And I'm really starving, Nick," she murmured, looking up at him, her blue eyes wide and miserable.

His expression softened. He tucked a strand of hair behind her ear.

She didn't realize how alluring her huge blue eyes were behind their mask of glass. She moistened her lips with the tip of a pink tongue.

Nick inhaled sharply. "I'll see if the kitchen is still serving. Do you know that it's almost midnight?" He started to get to his feet, hesitated, then sat down again. "Or would you rather get out of here?" he murmured huskily. He had turned toward her, one arm across the back of her chair, and his broad shoulders hid her from the rest of the group. His eyes held her mesmerized. "We're starting early in the morning."

"Are you angry with me?" she asked in a small voice.

"Now why would you think that?" He smiled slowly. Her blue eyes lowered to fix on the pulse in his throat.

"Because there's a spot right here that has been throbbing like mad ever since you came in." She put a finger to it to keep it in focus and rested her head against the muscular arm behind her.

Nick seemed to be holding his breath. His eyes burned across her face.

What was wrong with her? Her thoughts refused to behave. She longed for the arm behind her to move, to gather her closer. Raising her eyes to his mouth, she sighed, unable to banish the aching need to feel those lips on hers.

He didn't move as she traced a line with her finger up over his chin to his mouth. Her eyes lifted to his, and at the darkening look there her heart began to race.

"What's wrong with me?" she asked him lazily. Her hand fell to her lap to be picked up firmly by Nick's.

"Let's go," he said, hauling her to her feet.

At first Steven protested their leaving, but he gave in without too much argument in the face of Nick's grim determination.

Toni fumbled in her purse and gave Steven's keys to Sam. "Don't let him drive home, Sam."

"Don't worry, we'll both take a cab," Sam smiled. "Have fun!" He leered at the two of them.

Toni looked around at the knowing glances directed at her.

"Oh, no, it's not like that, Sam," she tried to protest. "He's my—"

"Let's go, Toni." Nick put a proprietory arm around her shoulder and steered her away through the crowd before she could explain.

When they were on the street the quiet enfolded her like a blanket.

Nick led her to a car, a blue Lincoln, and helped her into the front seat. Toni melted into the plush cushions and closed her eyes. She didn't ask where they were going. It didn't seem to matter as long as she was with him.

He drove for a while before stopping in front of an all-night delicatessen. When he opened the car to get out, the overhead light shone in Toni's eyes and she blinked. "I'll be right back. Just sit still," Nick ordered gently and she nodded, smiling sleepily up at him.

He returned in only a few minutes with a paper bag in one hand. He started the car again and Toni drifted back into her happy daze. She was with Nick and everything was fine.

It had begun to rain. The windshield wipers swept back and forth in rhythm with her pulse. Heavy eyelids closed, her long lashes resting lightly on her cheeks.

Nick had parked the car, and Toni managed to rouse herself to look around. They were in front of her apartment building. She subsided again into her peaceful cocoon.

"Where are your keys, Toni?"

She heard his deep voice as a rumble under her ear. "Umm?" Her cheek was nestled against something hard, covered with something incredibly soft and sleek. She put up a hand next to her cheek and ran her fingers across the sensuous material.

"I like that, darling, but don't you think we'd better go inside?" a husky voice demanded.

Toni tilted her head back and slowly opened her eyes.

Nick's face was inches away. His arm was around her shoulder, and her fingers were splayed across his chest.

There was something nagging at her. She frowned, trying to remember what it was. Something was wrong, but the wine had clouded her thinking, and whatever it was escaped her completely.

Nick's dark eyes roamed over her face, lingering on her lips. Slowly he lowered his head and the firm masculine mouth closed over hers. His lips were cool; experimentally they moved across her mouth tasting, sampling. The exploration was infinitely gentle, as though he relished her flavor. "I've wanted to do that for so very long," he whispered, his breath warm against her lips.

Toni felt as though her body had broken into a thousand tiny fragments, each one glittering and shining. "I wondered what it would be like to kiss you," she admitted in a small voice.

Lifting his head, Nick searched her wondering eyes. With an impatient movement he pulled the glasses from her nose and slid them across the dashboard. Her lips opened on a tiny gasp, and he covered them again with his, this time expanding the sensations. The arm at her shoulder stroked down to her waist to lift her closer. His other hand came up to tangle in her hair, holding her head still for his erotic search. His tongue probed the sweetness of her lips, her teeth, her tongue. This kiss was tender but demanding, too, leaving her floating somewhere above her body, helpless to deny him.

Dragging his mouth away with a deep shudder, he buried his face in the curve of her neck. "Give me your keys," he murmured hoarsely.

"What?" Toni didn't understand.

"Your keys!" Suddenly he pushed her away, holding her shoulders. His fingers gripped her tightly.

Toni shook her head and groped for her bag. She handed him the key ring.

Impatiently he opened the car door and got out, then going around to the passenger side, opened the door and pulled her out, ignoring the light rain. He reached for the paper bag. When they were in the elevator, Nick pushed the button and turned to look at her. She was lost in his eyes, vulnerable in a way that she had never been before. Still holding her hand, he steered her to the door of her apartment and gave her the bag to hold while he unlocked it. The muscle in his jaw was working again.

Toni went through the door first and stood looking around her. She had left only one small lamp burning in her apartment. It gave a soft circle of light, but it was enough to see by, so she didn't turn on any more. She dropped onto the sofa and, slipping out of her shoes, curled her feet under her.

"Don't go to sleep on me yet! You have to help eat these lobster rolls."

"Wonderful! I love lobster rolls," she murmured with a sleepy smile. Her head lolled lazily against the back of the sofa.

He sat beside her and opened the bag. There were napkins and two cups of coffee in Styrofoam cups, as well as the savory rolls. Nick took the plastic top from one coffee cup and gave her the container. "Can you hold that?"

"Certainly I can!" she said indignantly and lifted her head to glare at him. "What are you insinuating?" She curled both hands around the cup.

"I'm not insinuating! You, my darling girl, are soused!" He shook his head with a tolerant quirk of his lips.

At his use of the endearment, Toni jumped and a few drops of the hot coffee spilled onto her leg.

"You see what I mean? Did it burn you?"

"No, it's not that hot! And don't call me your darling girl! You're my almost-brother!" She sipped the black coffee. Brother? Was that the nagging thought? Nick wasn't her brother—she didn't have a brother. She shrugged.

He handed her a napkin and a lobster roll. "That's funny. I don't feel at all brotherly," he said, avoiding her eyes.

Toni ignored his remark and took a bite of the delicious roll. She chewed slowly, and then even more slowly. "That was very good, thank you. And now I think I'd like to go to sleep," she said with deliberate dignity. It was becoming more and more difficult to hold her eyes open.

"Sleep? You've only had one bite!"

Toni's head dropped back to rest on the cushion. "I know, but I'm so very sleepy, Nick," she slurred.

Nick quickly took the coffee and roll from her limp fingers. He set them on the table and encircled her with his arm, pulling her head over to rest against his chest. "Are you, sweetheart?" He chuckled. His other arm came around and he laced his fingers together, enclosing her in a warm circle.

Her fingers stroked over the deliciously soft cashmere. "This is nice." She snuggled against him and her eyes drooped contentedly.

"It is, isn't it?" Something in his voice caused her to look up at him. The expression in his eyes was hard to read. He was amused, she could see that, but there was something else there, too. "Would you kiss me again?" she whispered.

The white teeth flashed in a grin of masculine confidence. "I fully intend to."

Her heavy lids were almost closed, but her eyes followed his descending mouth until it closed over hers. He tasted her lips gently, lifted his head fractionally, and then tasted again. Suddenly he lifted her across his lap with a swiftness that left her even more befuddled. His mouth became sensual and hungry. One hand came up to thread through the tawny strands of her hair, forcing her head closer. The other shaped her breast with its palm.

Toni gasped at the sensations that raced along her nerve ends, and he took advantage of her open mouth to thrust his tongue against hers. The kiss was seductive and determined. There was nothing tender about it. Nick's hold on himself had slipped and he was deliberately arousing her, demanding a response.

Wave after wave of overwhelming emotion threatened to drown her. She clung to him as the only solid thing in a twisting tossing world. She was spinning helplessly in a whirlpool of ardent feeling. "Nick...oh, Nick," she murmured when he finally lifted his head.

He buried his face in the fragrance of her hair, taking in a deep shuddering breath. "Toni...oh, Toni," he mocked unsteadily. "You know what's happening to us, don't you?" he said against her ear.

"I don't know anything except I've never felt like this before." She hid her face in his neck.

"How do you feel?" She sensed his smile.

"Like I'm swimming in the middle of a hurricane," she whispered against his skin.

He gave a deep chuckle. His hand reluctantly left her breast to lift her chin, so that he could taste the parted moistness of her lips again.

"And I can't touch my toes to the bottom," she continued, rambling. "And...and...."

"And?"

"I've had too much wine." She snuggled sleepily against him again.

His arms tightened for a moment. "Yes, you have and I'm grateful for it."

She leaned back to look with wide eyes into his amused face. "I don't ever have more than one glass," she assured him with dignity. Then she frowned. "Grateful? What are you talking about?"

Nick traced her lips with a finger. "You lost those strong inhibitions for a while. I might never have broken through that reserve you surround yourself with otherwise. I had to know, darling. These have been the longest two weeks of my life.''

Toni tried to make sense out of what he was saying, but sleep made her eyelids heavy and her brain refused to function. Her head dropped against his shoulder. ''Tomorrow. I'll think tomorrow.''

Nick got to his feet with her in his arms. ''Don't go to sleep yet!'' He strode through to her bedroom and once there, set her on her feet, keeping one arm around her waist. ''Where are your pajamas?'' he asked, looking around the tiny room.

Toni rose to her full height. ''I don't sleep in them,'' she said proudly.

''Wha...at?''

She giggled at his expression. ''I told you! I sleep in very sexy teddies.''

He pulled her close with a growl. ''Oh, you do, do you? For whom?''

''For nobody, yet!'' she teased, tilting her head to the side to look up at him.

He shook his head with a rueful smile. ''Well, where are the sexy teddies?''

''In that drawer.'' She pointed and Nick let her go to pull at the brass knobs of a maple dresser.

He fumbled around among the scented lace. ''My God!'' he uttered, holding up a little bit of nothing before he stuffed it back in the drawer. Finally he found something that satisfied him, and he thrust it into her arms. ''Here! Go into the bathroom and put this on.''

She pouted. ''I don't want that! Nervy only gave

it to me in case the building caught on fire."

"Put it on! Or else something else is going to catch fire—namely me!" He turned her toward the bathroom door.

"But, Nick—"

"Scat!" He gave her a push.

When Toni came out five minutes later she was enveloped to her toes in demure white dimity with blue ribbons. The gown had a drawstring neckline outlined by a wide eyelet ruffle. The ruffle was repeated at the wrist and fell gracefully across her hands. "I feel like granny in this," she complained. When Nick didn't answer she looked at him.

He watched her for a long time before he answered in a husky voice. "You look like a beautiful young woman on her wedding night," he murmured. "Infinitely desirable."

There was a look in his eyes that caused her knees to collapse, and gripping the post for dear life, she sank onto the edge of the bed. "Nick?" she questioned weakly.

He swerved away from her gaze, running the fingers of one hand through his hair. "Oh, hell! I've got to get out of here," he muttered almost to himself. He bent to swing her feet up, then tucked her in under the covers he had turned down. He leaned over, one hand on each side of her head. "I'll call to wake you up at seven." He kissed her briefly. "We'll have breakfast with Aunt Lydia and then drive to the Cape. Okay?"

"Okay," she whispered, her heavy lids closing again. She felt his lips on her eyes, and then his warm breath filled her mouth. But when she lifted her arms and would have responded he dragged her hands away and tucked them under the covers. "Good night, my... Toni."

"Good night, Nick."

6

AT SEVEN O'CLOCK the next morning the telephone rang. Toni groaned and rolled to the other side of the double bed, pulling the pillow over her pounding head. "Shh," she whispered, but whoever was on the other end was persistent. Finally she rolled back to reach for the receiver. As she dragged it toward her ear, she heard a click and then the brash buzzing of a dial tone. Relieved, she hung up and got out of bed. She made her way to the bathroom and fumbled for the aspirin bottle. After shaking out two white tablets she thirstily drank a large glass of water. Why did she have such a headache? Oh, yes, the wine. And what else? Something teased the back of her mind, but she ignored it and climbed into bed, sinking swiftly once again into deep sleep.

WARM LIPS LEISURELY FEATHERED HER CHEEK, moved lazily to her ear, then down to nuzzle her neck. She was dreaming. It had to be a remote wonderful dream. A voice husky with passion whispered her name.

Toni sighed contentedly and lifted her arms to bury her fingers in thick springy hair. The drawstring ribbon of her gown was pulled free, and warm breath in the hollow between her breasts forced a small moan from her. "Oh, Nick," she murmured.

Strong arms lifted her pliant form to mold the soft curves against a hard masculine chest, even as firm lips parted her own to plunder the sweetness within.

She responded without hesitation. Restless hands moved across to measure the width of broad shoulders, then returned to relish the feel of muscles in the strong neck. Her body arched to exciting caresses along the length of her spine.

The mouth was dragged from hers, and she whimpered at the loss. Long fingers cradled her head against his chest. "You scared me when you didn't answer your phone," Nick said thickly.

"Was that you?" she asked still half-asleep.

"Who else were you expecting?" he growled against her temple.

"No one," she whispered dreamily. "I'm sorry."

"I'm glad I kept your keys. I'd hate to explain a broken door to your landlord."

Toni could hear the irregular beat off his heart under her ear. Impatiently she tilted her head back, and her lips found the pulse point in his throat.

"Oh, God, Toni!" Nick groaned. He lowered her to the pillow, and his lips hovered again over hers. "Open your eyes," he ordered.

Slowly she lifted her heavy lids. Her gray blue eyes had darkened to midnight. The arms around his neck slackened slightly in confusion.

"Are you awake?" he asked against her lips.

Her nostrils were filled with the male scent of him.

His hair was damp under her hands. "I...I'm not sure," she whispered. "I may still be dreaming." She was hypnotized by the desire in his eyes.

Then he was kissing her again, deeply and with a consuming hunger. He had lowered himself on the bed to lie beside her, but now he rolled over, pinning her beneath his hard length while his mouth ravaged her lips with a yearning sweeping passion.

He ground her hips into the mattress beneath them with an exciting movement that left her stunningly aware of his desire, his need for her. His arms crushed her to him. "Oh, Toni! My little Toni!" His voice was a harsh rasp. "For two weeks I've thought of nothing but holding you in my arms like this. Kissing you, touching you. I could have killed that puppy last night when I walked into Fridays and saw him pawing you!" he growled.

Toni was barely hovering on the edge of consciousness. What had he called her? His little.... "No! No, Nick! Let me go!" she cried, struggling to save herself from her own arousal, from drowning under the stimulation of his touch. She pushed at him, frantic now, and his arms loosened slightly, but he still held her.

Nick lifted his head to look again into her eyes. Time seemed to stand still.

The emotions of embarrassment and overwhelming regret warred. She had given her feelings away—last night and again this morning. What had come over her? How could she have done this? She tore her gaze away and turned her head into his shoulder. "Please, Nick. Let me go," she begged. There was a strident break in her voice.

Nick regarded her bent head. With a hand that shook slightly he smoothed her tawny hair back from her face and tilted her chin up to search her eyes. A sad smile played across his lips as he sat up, then settled her back against the pillows. "I'll wait for you in the other room," he said huskily.

"Nick, I... I can't go with you today. I have an awful headache," she said, reaching for the first excuse, which just happened to be true.

"Yes, you are going," he stated harshly. "I knew you'd try to back out this morning, but I won't let you. Take some aspirin!"

"Nick, please...." She hung her head in shame. "Please," she whispered.

"No! We have to talk, Toni!" His voice when he spoke again was lowered. "Something is there between us and we're going to look at it."

"No! Oh, no... what have I done?" she cried.

"Nothing. You haven't done anything, do you hear?" He gave her a little shake.

Hating herself for her weakness, she felt a tear streak her cheek. With a groan Nick pulled her into his arms, rocking her, murmuring soothing words in her ear as one might comfort a child. His plaid wool shirt was abrasive against her cheek. "You haven't knowingly done anything, sweetheart, and neither have I. It just happened." He lifted a hand to cradle the side of her face. His thumb touched her lips and she shivered.

"Give me today, Toni," he demanded. "Let me try to find a solution."

She looked at him, her eyes wanting to hope, to trust him, but the days when Toni let others assume the responsibility for her happiness were long past. "There is no solution," she said in a throaty regretful voice. Angela, she thought. My own sister! Even if.... She stopped that thought before it could begin. There was no future for her and Nick. None.

"I had too much wine last night," she said, dropping her eyes.

"Look at me!" he demanded. She did. "Tell me with all honesty that what happened between us was because you had too much wine!" His somber eyes refused to release hers. "Or was it because for the last two weeks I've been as much on your mind as you've been on mine?"

She couldn't answer for a moment. Then she gave a ragged sigh. "It doesn't matter. It doesn't change anything, and there's no future in it."

Angrily his mouth subdued the protest on her lips. There was no gentleness now. He was laying deliberate claim to her. When he lifted his head he was pale. "Today is our day out of time, Toni. We're going to spend it together. The future will work itself out, but today is ours," he pronounced huskily. He let her go and stood up, towering over her, hands thrust into the pockets of his jeans. "Now, get dressed," he ordered. "Wear jeans and bring along a warm jacket." He left the room, jerking the door closed behind him.

Toni dragged herself out of bed and into the bathroom. Standing under the stinging spray of the shower, she tried to reconstruct her defenses against her powerful attraction for the man who waited in her living room. But, as she soaped her body, the memory of the touch of his hands, the masterful message of his mouth haunted her.

Her sister's fiancé! She groaned aloud as she turned off the shower and reached for a towel. Her dear and loving sister who trusted her! How could she have let herself do this? She, who was always in control of her life, her mind, her emotions, suddenly had lost all levelheadedness, all perspective. He made her forget the values she had grown up with. All he had to do was look at her, and she was transported to an unreal place. Nick had said there was something between them. He was obviously as drawn to her as she was to him, but he was an experienced worldly man. What he felt for her was probably only a physical attraction, while her feelings went disastrously deeper. She had tried, for two weeks she had tried, to put him out of her mind—because inside she knew that when she did finally examine her feelings she would have to admit to herself just how deeply they went.

Toni dressed quickly in white jeans and a pale blue sweater. She twisted her hair into its familiar bun and touched her lips with gloss. With a shaking hand she reached for the doorknob just as there was a sharp knock.

"Toni?" Nick called through the closed door.

For a moment Toni rested her forehead against the

white panel in front of her. It was cool and soothing to her warm skin. Then she straightened, took a deep breath and opened the door to face Nick.

He stood there looking at her, a strange sort of understanding in his eyes. "Are you ready?"

Toni straightened her shoulders and met his gaze calmly. "I would rather not go with you, Nick," she said resolutely. "I don't think it's wise. In fact, it's just plain stupid."

"Stupid!" His hands circled her waist and pulled her toward him. At the first touch of his thighs against her Toni stiffened. His eyes dropped deliberately to her lips before returning to her eyes, noting the angry flush rising in her cheeks. "You're probably right, but I'm just selfish enough to insist," he answered adamantly, stepping back for her to enter the living room. "This feeling we have for each other is not going to go away just because we decide to ignore it. Where is your jacket?"

"Please!" She was almost pleading now. "Let me stay here."

Firm hands on her shoulders turned her toward him. One move to tilt up her chin. His own expression was grim but determined. "I can imagine very few things I would ever be able to refuse you, Toni, but this is one of them. Now, where is your jacket?"

Shoulders slumped in uncharacteristic defeat, she turned to the small coat closet and took out a white windbreaker trimmed in the same pale blue as her sweater. She reached for her purse and walked on wooden legs out of the apartment.

After a short silent drive, Nick turned the Lincoln into an alley behind a block of older, substantial homes. A carriage house had been converted into a garage.

Toni shivered when they went from bright sunshine into the windowless enclosure. It took a moment for her eyes to adjust, then she reached for the door handle.

Without touching her, Nick held her with his voice. "I want to prepare you, Toni," he said gravely.

Her eyes flew to his, accusing. "You haven't told her?" she asked indignantly.

Nick laughed hollowly. "Told her what?"

Toni couldn't answer. Her eyes fell to the hands twisted together in her lap.

"No, I haven't told her anything except that you're Angela's sister."

At the mention of her sister's name, guilt stabbed through her, but she lifted her chin to a defiant tilt.

"But Aunt Lydia is a very perceptive lady. She never married and I'm her only relative, so she knows me well." He sighed. "When you didn't come to dinner last night...well, I'm afraid, my impatience was obvious."

"What?" Toni asked, not understanding.

Nick raked restless fingers through his hair and shook his head. "Nothing! What I wanted to prepare you for is the fact that my aunt is in a wheelchair. She hasn't walked since she was twenty-one years old."

Toni looked at him then, the expression in her eyes

softening sympathetically. "Oh, Nick! How awful for her!"

He chuckled. "Your sympathy would be wasted on Aunt Lydia. The accident that took away her mobility hasn't slowed her down at all, as you'll see. Let's go in."

They entered a tiny walled garden through a heavy wooden gate off the alley. Nick's hand rested lightly at her waist. When she tried to move away his fingers tightened warningly.

Nick's Aunt Lydia welcomed them with a warm smile. Her eyes were the same warm brown as Nick's, although slightly clouded at the moment. Her beautiful silver hair was cut short and curled softly about her face. She wore a sweater the color of rich burgundy and gray wool slacks—no blanket to cover the useless legs for her. Her feet were tiny and clad in gray suede espadrilles as though any minute she might hop up and walk. "My dear, I'm so happy to meet you. Please forgive me for not getting up, but as you see...." She indicated the wheelchair.

Toni crossed to where she sat and took the outstretched hand. "I'm happy to meet you, Miss Trabert. Thank you for having me," she answered sincerely. Lydia must have been almost sixty, but Toni was unprepared for the vitality emanating from the tiny form. Nick was right! It was easy to regret the awful circumstances that had put her in the wheelchair, but impossible to pity this spirited vibrant woman.

"Call me Lydia, please, Toni. Nick, would you tell

Jane that she can serve breakfast now?" Lydia's words were accompanied by a smile, and Nick disappeared into the house. "Sit down here, Toni." She indicated a patio chair with a bright yellow cushion next to her.

Toni looked around the garden. Yellow tulips bordered one wall of the quiet retreat. A huge red maple shaded three-quarters of the small lawn providing what, in the summer, would be a cool oasis. Today the white wrought-iron table and chairs had been placed to take advantage of the warm sunshine.

"What a lovely garden!" Toni said. She turned to meet the searching eyes of Nick's aunt and sensed that this observant woman had recognized something amiss. She smiled shyly, not knowing that her own huge blue eyes held a hint of fear.

Lydia had been studying her closely. She seemed to reach some sort of conclusion about Toni, for she relaxed visibly and looked around with a smile. "Thank you. It's my own little Eden. I love to be outdoors and spring is my favorite time of year. It's always such a happy surprise when the first crocus bloom appears after a hard winter." Lydia breathed in the clear air and looked at Toni again. "I'm glad the rain has stopped and won't spoil your trip today."

To avoid discussion of the trip, Toni asked, "Have you ever spent a spring in Atlanta?"

Lydia laughed. "The second year Nick was there, he insisted I come down for the Dogwood Festival. He said, 'You just won't believe it,' and I didn't! It was breathtakingly beautiful. I'll never forget that year. When I returned to Boston there were still patches of snow in the parks, so I enjoyed two springs, one there, and a later one here."

Nick returned, followed shortly by a plump gray-haired woman rolling a tea cart.

"Mmm. That smells delicious. Jane, this is Nick's friend, Toni Grey," Lydia said, then turned to Toni. "Jane and her husband, Howard, take care of me. I couldn't exist without them."

Jane sniffed. "Ha!" She smiled fondly at her employer. "You'd find a way."

While Lydia poured coffee into delicate china cups Jane removed covers from platters of bacon, eggs and a fruit compote.

Nick handed a plate to Toni. They helped themselves from the cart while the older woman served Lydia.

Toni was sampling from the fruit compote when Lydia said, "Nick, you're very quiet this morning."

His gaze was startled away from where it rested on Toni's bent head. He sat down abruptly on the other side of his aunt. "Sorry, Aunt Lydia. I was thinking."

"Certainly you were!" she said cheerfully.

Nick's head jerked up and his eyes narrowed, but Lydia had turned to Toni. "I hope you'll enjoy your trip today, Toni. The house you're going to see has been in our family for three generations. My great-grandfather built it as a summer home."

"House?" Toni asked blankly. "Nick didn't say where we were going."

"He didn't?" Lydia raised an eyebrow. "He probably expected you just to go along, no questions asked. He's always been a bit of a bully when it comes to getting his way." The dimples in her cheeks belied her criticism. She obviously doted on her nephew.

Nick grinned. "Only when it's for your own good, Aunt Lydia." He picked up a piece of toast and reached for the crystal jam jar. "Who's the fourth place for?" he asked, indicating the unused place setting at the table. He spooned rich red strawberry jam onto his plate.

"John's coming."

"Good! I'll get a firsthand critique of my lecture, and if I know John he'll rip me to pieces." The red concoction was spread onto a wedge of toast.

Their conversation had gone over her head as Toni watched Nick's large hands and remembered.... She forced her attention back to Lydia. "Where is the house?" she asked.

"It's in Harwich Port overlooking Nantucket Sound. The house has been rented ever since Nick moved to Atlanta. I didn't want it to stand empty. But now...." Lydia suddenly seemed at a loss. She gave a vague wave of her hand. "Well, anyway, the tenants moved out a few weeks ago, and I wanted Nick to arrange for some repairs and remodeling."

While they were eating Nick reminded his aunt, "You were going to make me a list of things you wanted done, Aunt Lydia."

"Yes. I did that and also jotted down the names of people who have done work for us in the past. The general contractor will meet you there at twelve o'clock. His name is Roy Williams. I want...." Her words trailed off as a booming voice reached them through the French doors of the house.

"Never mind, Jane. I know my way." A very, very different Professor Winter appeared.

Toni's jaw dropped at the sight. He was dressed in casual slacks and a well-worn tweed jacket over a yellow sports shirt. Yellow, for heaven's sake!

"Good morning, Lydia! Nick my boy! Good to see you! And here's Miss Grey." A beautiful smile lit his face as he stuck out a hand. "Nick, my boy, you haven't lost your touch! Congratulations. She's lovely and smart. I couldn't believe your luck when Lydia told me that you were engaged to Miss Grey from Atlanta. How fortuitous that she just happens to be my best contracts student. You two will make quite a pair." He turned to Toni, who had gotten to her feet. "How are you, my dear? I hope you'll allow me a little familiarity on this more social occasion."

Toni found her hand swallowed up in his, an arm around her shoulders. She was dumbfounded not only by his hearty demeanor, but by his assumption that she was Nick's fiancée. Lydia must not have told him about Angela. In fact, it was strange that Lydia had not even mentioned Angela at all.

Lydia was nervously trying to interrupt the steady flow of conversation, but she might as well have been a gnat buzzing around an elephant.

Nick, with an unholy smile of amusement on his face, came around the table to detach Toni from a bear hug. "Hands off, John. I know you! You'd try to steal her! Toni, you know the staid and stuffy Professor Winter, deeply immersed in the law. Let me present my godfather, John, the old lecher!"

John Winter assumed a look of mock resentment. "Steal her, indeed!" Then he twinkled at Toni. "Although if you're smart, my dear, you'll think twice before you marry this rounder!"

Toni gaped at him. Nick wasn't helping a bit! While Lydia fluttered her hands trying to get his attention. "John...."

"No, Lydia, I didn't forget the papers," he said, misunderstanding her agitation. "Here they are." He drew some papers from his jacket pocket. "Well, children, what did you think of your wedding present? Lydia wanted the deed to read 'for one dollar and other considerations,' such as filling the house with children! How's that for a contract?" He laughed heartily, into dead silence.

Toni's heart pounded in her ears, but she forced a laugh into her voice. "Professor Winter...John, I'm not Nick's fiancée. I'm her sister."

A flush of red lit his face. "Oh! I'm so sorry, my dear. And I gather I've let the cat out of the bag, haven't I?" He looked at Lydia, chastened.

"Yes, you have!" she said angrily. "For a lawyer you aren't very discreet!" She looked from Toni to Nick, who hadn't moved. Her teeth worried her bottom lip, but she didn't speak.

Nick's gaze was riveted on Toni. She met it with a sharp lift of her chin.

"Let's finish our breakfast," Lydia added nervously. "Would anyone like more coffee?"

"I think we'd better be on our way, Aunt Lydia," Nick said in an even voice, but the pulse in his throat was throbbing angrily again.

When they were in the car Toni demanded to be taken home.

"No! You're going with me!" He pulled the Lincoln out of the alley and eased into the traffic.

"I don't want to go!" she fumed.

"Well, by damned, you're going! So be quiet!" he roared.

Toni sniffed.

"I didn't know about the house," Nick told her, struggling for control. "Look, Toni...John didn't mean to embarrass you. He's a fine fellow. Don't hold it against him."

"I'm not—I'm holding it against you! You shouldn't have taken me there in the first place. I'm not your financée—Angela is!"

Nick's hands clenched on the wheel until his knuckles were white. The muscle in his jaw hardened. "Do you really think I can marry Angela now?" he asked in a frozen voice.

"You have to. You can't hurt her like that!"

"Don't you think I would hurt her more if I married her with this between you and me?" he asked quietly.

"There is nothing between us! Nothing! And there will never be!" Her voice broke on a sob. She put a shaking hand to her temple. Her head had begun to throb again.

"Don't lie to yourself, Toni! Or to me! I feel as badly about this as you do."

Toni didn't have anything to say. She gave him a resentful glare and turned to look sightlessly out the window. The rest of this day promised to be as disastrous as the last half hour had been. If only Nick would let her go home, be by herself, she could give way to the pit of misery around her heart.

Nick reached out and switched on the radio to an FM station playing classical music. The piano strains of Paderewski's "*Minuet*" filled the car. "Relax, Toni," Nick ordered. "Take a nap if you can. We'll be there in about an hour."

Grateful not to have to talk, she leaned her pounding head against the back of the seat and closed her eyes. What kind of a person was she? To have caused the breakup of her own sister's engagement! Grief for herself and for Angela flooded her heart, but her eyes were dry, and she was thankful.

Paderewski gave way to Chopin and Toni dwelled for a long time in a half dream of melancholy. The powerful car ate up the miles. As the notes of the beautiful piano music soothed her troubled heart she finally succumbed to a troubled sleep.

Angela was lovely in a bridal gown of satin and tulle. The veil fell from a crown to her feet. But she was coming up the aisle, not down, on the arm of their father. Agnes was on her other side. The three of them were surrounded with a misty golden aura. They pointed accusingly at Toni. Their voices were harsh. "You have destroyed any love we felt for you.

Don't ever let us see you again!" They turned their backs, and Angela's veil spread and grew to cover the floor of the church. Toni tried to reach them, to explain, but her feet kept tangling in the folds of the tulle, until she gave up trying to walk and crawled toward them. "Please, please look at me. Daddy! Angela! Agnes! Oh, daddy please see me," she pleaded.

"Shh. It's all right. Darling, wake up."

Toni opened her eyes. Nick was holding her, stroking her tumbled hair back from her face, removing the rest of the pins and putting them in his pocket.

"I was dreaming?" she asked him shakily.

"Just a bad dream," he reassured her.

Toni drew a shaky breath of relief. Then she realized that it wasn't a dream at all. It was happening. She sat up straight with a jerk.

Nick rested his arm along the seat back and watched her hands lift to push her hair away from her face.

"May I have my pins back?"

"No," he answered shortly.

She dropped her arms and turned to stare at him. "Why?" she asked. "What difference does it make?"

He looked down into her eyes still clouded by the dream. Moving his hand beneath the heavy swath of hair on her nape, he began to stroke the soft skin there. "Because, my darling girl, you are a fraud!" His voice was husky. His hand continued its rhythmic massage while his other arm went to her waist to turn her toward him. He looked into her eyes. "Those glasses you wore were plain glass."

"Where are my glasses?" she demanded, trying unsuccessfully to release herself from the powerful magnetic force of his gaze. Delicious sensations traveled to her nerve ends at his sensuous touch.

"At the bottom of the Charles River where I threw them last night after I left you." He bent his head to touch her lips lightly but firmly with his own. Then he went on, "And when you pull your hair back in that ridiculous bun, you expose the most delicious curve in your neck that just begs to be nibbled." He moved her hair aside and suited his actions to his words. "I don't want anyone else to be tempted by it."

His warm breath on her skin made her quiver. "Don't do that!" she ordered, trying with her head to deny him access to the sensitive spot.

Nick raised his head and looked at her with pretended innocence. "You don't like it?" he teased.

"It makes no difference whether I like it or not!" she said shakily.

"Well, then . . . ." He resumed his exploration. The arm around her shoulder tightened. The other hand strayed up to tenderly caress her breast. "And if you think that tailored clothes hide those sexy curves of yours . . . ."

"Nick, please." Toni struggled to be free of the drugging sensations he was causing. She pushed at him. "Why have you stopped the car?" she demanded.

Nick sighed reluctantly as he let his arms drop and

leaned across to open her door. "We're here," he said with a grin.

Toni looked up at the house. Her brow cleared at the sight. It was magnificent!

The huge clapboard structure, set in the middle of a wide expanse of lawn, was a weathered gray with white louvered shutters flanking each tall window. A wide veranda with a white railing circled the house on the first floor, and another one stretched across the upper floor facing the ocean.

She got out of the car, grateful to escape his nearness in the confined space, and looked back along the curved drive. The road was hidden from view by shrubbery and long-needle pine trees. Nestled into the copse of trees was what looked to be a gate house of gray stone.

Toni's eyes returned to the big house in front of her. What a perfectly beautiful spot!

Silently Nick came around the car and took her arm. "Do you like it?"

"Like it! Nick, it's beautiful!" she answered with a trace of wistfulness in her voice.

"It is, isn't it? I've always loved this place. When I was a child we spent every summer here."

Toni let herself be led up the steps to wait while Nick unlocked the back door. They walked directly into a large old-fashioned kitchen. There was a small fireplace in one corner, and in the center of the floor was an oak trestle table surrounded by eight oak chairs. The walls were painted a soft yellow. Toni stood looking around her, enthralled.

"Why don't you explore while I bring in the picnic basket?" Jane had handed them the basket along with Nick's briefcase when they left Lydia's house.

Toni turned sparkling eyes to him, her troubles momentarily forgotten. "May I?"

"Sure. You...."

"What?" she questioned.

"Nothing." He smiled down at her tenderly. "You go ahead, but don't get lost!"

7

TONI WATCHED NICK LEAVE and pivoted in anticipation of exploring this marvelous old house. It was chilly inside, so she kept her jacket on, burying her hands in the flannel-lined pockets.

On the ground floor was a living room, a less formal parlor, a dining room, a study and a music room. There was a fireplace in each one, and all the rooms opened onto the veranda. Her sneaker-clad feet barely made a sound on the hardwood floors. Toni paused at the front door, looking out across the water of Nantucket Sound. She could imagine a hot summer day, the house full of children, laughing and playing in the sand and surf, returning periodically to the shade of the veranda for a cool drink. Lemonade. For a house like this it would have to be lemonade! She smiled to herself and started up the stairs. On the second floor were three bedrooms, each with its own bath, and a master suite overlooking the beach. The third floor housed a nursery, a huge playroom on one side of a hall, and three small bedrooms on the other. At the end of the hall was another bedroom with a private bath, presumably quarters for a nurse. Toni lingered for a moment at the door of the playroom. There were bookshelves—toddler height—tiny tables and chairs and a wooden rocking horse with a bedraggled mop for a tail.

Until this moment Toni had been able to convince herself that she was enjoying a look at an interesting old house, but now a new shaft of pain pierced her. Nick had played here as a child. His tiny hands had turned the pages in the books. He had probably ridden the rocking horse with a vengeance. Someday his children would play here, too.

Toni whirled away and started toward the steps. She had to get out of here!

"Toni!" The voice came from the stairwell below her.

As she reached the second-floor landing she paused to catch her breath.

"Toni," he called again. "Where are you?"

She moved toward the stairs so that he could see her, but she couldn't answer. Her throat was dry.

Nick had one foot on the first stair, but when he saw her start down he backed to wait for her, a smile on his face. He had discarded his jacket, and the plaid shirt emphasized the width of his shoulders. His hair was rumpled, and she longed to smooth it away from his forehead. His gaze took in her pale face, her hesitant steps. Slowly he held out his arms. "Come here to me," he ordered gently.

She stopped halfway down. "No," she whispered, shaking her head when what she desperately wanted was to be enfolded in those welcoming arms.

"You came down the steps and into my arms once. Couldn't you do it again?" he urged huskily.

Toni giggled nervously and took another stair. "Do you mean you want me to knock you flat?" she asked, trying to lighten the atmosphere between them.

His eyes darkened and locked with hers. "You knock me flat every time I see you, every time I touch you." His voice became a mesmerizing sensation. "I haven't been able to think straight since I first lost myself in those beautiful blue eyes. Think with your heart, Toni, and not your mind. Forget everyone but me for today. Just once, do what your heart tells you." His arms were still open.

She hesitated. "Will you promise...."

Planting his fists on his hips, his anger erupted. "Hell, no! I'm not promising a damn thing! I'm in love with you, you blind idiot! I've tried to be patient with your innocence and guilt, but my patience is wearing thin," he raged. "You're a woman, Toni, not a child!"

Her eyes widened in wonderful disbelief. "You... you love me?"

He looked up at her and answered resolutely, "More than I ever thought it was possible to love anyone." Then he opened his arms again.

Toni took a stair, and then another. "Oh, Nick, this is wrong!" she whispered in anguish. But even as she told him that, told herself that, she was running down toward the haven, her arms reaching for him. They circled his neck, and his clamped around her waist to lift her off the last stair.

His mouth fastened hungrily on her parted lips. When he let her slide down the length of his body, his head lowered, too, never relinquishing its hold on her mouth.

Toni's fingers reveled in the feel of his hair. She was barely standing on tiptoe, but she arched toward his hard body, knowing that he wouldn't let her fall. Once she had wondered what it would be like to love someone so totally, so absolutely that there was no room for anyone else. Now she knew. She forgot Angela, her family, everything, in the protection of his arms.

His hands caressed her back, her hips, fitting her to his hard thighs. "I love you. Oh, my darling, I love you!"

Toni responded almost desperately, her hands touching his face and moving across the broad shoulders, then back again to grasp his neck, straining him closer.

Nick searched her face. Then he laughed, a triumphant joyful sound as he swept her up into his arms. He covered her face with kisses, her eyes, her nose, her cheeks as he carried her into the parlor and sat on a deep sofa with her across his lap. He unzipped her jacket with unsteady fingers. "I've built a fire. You won't need this. Besides, I like you in sweaters," he told her, grinning as he slipped the jacket off her shoulders and tossed it to the floor. Pulling her back into the warm circle of his arms, his mouth returned to hers. His tongue traced the outline of her moist lips; he nibbled, teased, toyed with them until, frustrated, Toni held his face still in her hands.

Her eyes glistened darkly through the thick screen of her lashes. What was it that made this man different from all other men she had known? She loved him, that was all that mattered. "Do what your heart tells you," he had said, and she was. For the moment there was no one in the world but the two of them, and her heart was soaring.

Nick allowed her to pull his head down until their lips met, allowed her the initiative for a moment before he took over. His arms tightened. The kiss became demanding, sensual.

Toni felt herself swimming fathoms deep in the passion he aroused. The hand at her back pushed under her sweater to roam over the bare skin underneath. She trembled at its burning touch across her shoulders and up to her nape.

Nick gave a great shuddering sigh as he finally dragged his mouth away. Sliding his hand down her back to curve around her hip, he lifted his head with an effort. With it's loving tenderness, his gaze penetrated her heart. When he spoke his voice was deep with emotion. "I'm like my father, Toni.... I've found my one great love. I knew it the first minute our eyes met, I think. I haven't been able to get my mind off you. But when I walked into that classroom yesterday and looked at you, it hit me like a sledgehammer." He laughed a little under his breath. His hands moved to her arms, massaging, caressing, but with a great effort he put her away from him. "I have no idea what kind of lecture I gave. All I could see was you."

Toni dropped her eyes to her hands resting against his chest. "I have no idea, either. I was hoping that someone in my group was taking notes." She lifted her eyes to his. They were bright with glowing ardor. "Because I didn't hear a word you said," she said softly.

"Darling?" His voice was hoarse with the unspoken question.

"I love you, too, Nick," she admitted and was instantly crushed to his chest. Her mouth blossomed under his masterful kiss. Beneath her hands she could feel his heart beating with a strong fast tempo. She wriggled her arms free to wind them around his neck, clinging to him.

As she curved closer, the slim hold he seemed to have on his control slipped. His restless hands moved feverishly over her hips, her waist, and up under her sweater to cup her breasts through the sheer lace bra.

She could feel them swelling, the nipples hardening under his firm stroke. She moaned deep in her throat. No one had ever touched her like this, set her on fire with a longing for a fulfillment she didn't know. What she was doing was insane. She knew that, but she could not deny the desire for him that burned through her. She forgot tomorrow in the warmth of his arms and fumbled with the buttons on his shirt. When they were free she pushed the sides back, baring his chest to her gaze. Her eyes lit with childlike fascination as she looked at him. His skin was tanned and smooth across his broad shoulders, but just beneath them a virile thatch of hair began. She put a palm to his chest, tentatively testing the sensation. The hair was surprisingly soft. She combed through it with her nails. Her lips curved in an unconsciously sensual smile as she drew tiny circles around the hard male nipples.

Nick had sat quietly under her exploration until that moment. He inhaled sharply, then took both her wrists in one hand, holding them against him, stilling their movement.

"Don't you want me to touch you?" she sighed.

"Oh, God, yes! But, darling...." His voice, which was always so strong, languished now into a love-blurred husky murmur.

"I want you to touch me, too," she whispered. The fires were there inside, blazing, and there was only one way to extinguish them.

But Nick was going to give her one more chance. He pulled her into an embrace of tender passion and tucked her head under his chin. "I love you, and I want you so desperately that I'll explode if I don't feel you under me soon!" His arms convulsed, and he had to take a long deep breath before he could continue. "But, my darling, I want you to be very sure."

His heart was pounding. She could feel it under her fingers, and her own pulse raced to match its rhythm. She tilted her head back so that he could see her face when she answered with the same words. "I love you, Nick. I want you and I am very sure."

His eyes were alive with a brilliant, shining, almost worshipful luster. "Love is a pale word for what I feel for you, Antonia Grey," he said. He stood up, holding her effortlessly against his heart, and strode out of the room and up the stairs.

Toni locked her arms around his neck and held his eyes. Her own were unafraid, expectant.

When he reached the doorway of the master bedroom that she'd explored earlier he let her legs swing to the floor. "Come here," he said unnecessarily, since he was leading her to the huge four-poster bed with its white candlewick spread. He sat on the edge and pulled her between his legs. His arms encircled her waist, and he buried his face in the softness of her sweater.

With an almost protective action she cradled him to her and laid her cheek on his head. Her hair fell like a curtain around his shoulders as she slid her fingers inside the collar of his open shirt. His muscles bunched under her lazy exploration. His reaction to her touch fostered a feeling she had never experienced before, a feeling of power over another, which was at once exhilarating and humbling.

Very slowly, very gently his hands began to move over her back, drawing large circles from her shoulders to her waist. Wherever they touched they warmed, leaving her body relaxed and pliable. They dropped sensuously to cup her rounded bottom and then slid around to the sides of her hips to move her back a few inches.

He looked up at her, a half-smile quirking his mouth. "I've dreamed of this, in my bed, alone. I've dreamed of undressing you, of seeing you as naked as I thought you were that night in the moonlight."

Her voice was but a thin thread of sound. "What must you have thought of me?"

"I was beyond thought, my love," he whispered, as his eyes dropped to the curves of her breasts and then to the snap of her jeans. He put out a hand to release it.

She caught her breath as he slid the zipper down and folded back the sides.

His warm breath caressed the sensitive skin of her flat stomach. His head moved as he planted soft kisses all across the silken surface. His tongue delved into the delicate hollow of her navel, and she almost collapsed against him.

"Oh, Nick!" she cried. Her knees would no longer support her, and only the strength in his hands as they moved to the back of her thighs held her erect.

He let her sit, then, on one of his knees, while he stripped the sweater over her head and tossed it to the floor. His black eyes devoured the full thrust of her ripe breasts against the sheer veil of her bra. It was quickly disposed of, and he lifted her onto the bed behind him. He tugged her jeans over her hips and they, too, went flying.

A thin film of perspiration appeared on his brow when he reached for the final barrier. Very slowly, with almost painful deliberation, he eased the scrap of lace down her legs, his hands brushing with a feather touch her inner thighs, the back of her knees.

There was no such loitering as he tore the clothes from his own body. In only seconds he stood, looming over her, a magnificent male animal, with a hunger in his eyes that was only barely contained by the love that demanded he keep an iron-hard control of himself. With a hand on each side of her head he leaned down to cover her parted lips with a kiss of such profound adoration that it moved her almost to tears.

Toni reached for him, threading her fingers into his thick hair, letting her response speak, for the lump in her throat choked off all words.

"The reality is more than the dream, my darling," he murmured against her lips. "Your body is a beautiful miracle. Let me.... Oh, God!"

With a surge of passion she arched her body up to his, and the hoarse groan that escaped from his throat was lost in her mouth as she clung to him with a vehemence that cloaked the anxiety she felt about the unknown.

Nick was not deceived. "Slowly, my darling," he murmured. "I won't hurt you, I promise. Just relax, sweetheart." His voice calmed, soothed as his hands began to stroke with unhurried caresses. His thumbs scraped gently across her nipples, surprising a gasp from her. When his mouth opened over one rosy peak with a soft pulling motion she felt as though every sense, honed razor sharp, was collecting somewhere deep within her, collecting for a massive assault on her very being. With each exquisite touch at her breasts, her silken thighs, each moist hungry kiss, he brought her closer to the peak of ecstasy.

Toni whimpered, mindless, aching for fulfillment, and with a satisfied sigh Nick covered her body with his and joined them in tender union. "My love, my dearest love," he breathed against the soft skin of her neck, moving within her slowly at first, then with increasing tempo, until the primitive rhythm caught them both in its flow, hurling them into wave after wave of climactic, shuddering pleasure.

She cried his name at the moment of release.

Their bodies, damp and spent, nevertheless were still intimately entwined.

When she could breathe without fear that her heart would stop, Toni looked at him, her eyes filled with wonder.

His smile was soft, loving and she traced it with a finger. She opened her mouth to tell him how much she loved him when suddenly chimes rang out in the still empty house.

"Oh, hell!" Nick groaned, rolling away from her.

Toni's breathing was shallow. "Nick?" she whispered.

He ran a hand through his rumpled hair and lifted an arm to glance at his wristwatch. "It's Aunt Lydia's contractor, darling. I'm afraid, with the car parked outside, he won't go away." He leaned over to give her a sweet hungry kiss before getting to his feet. He pulled on his jeans and shirt, buttoning the shirt with fingers that were shaking, and thrust the ends into his jeans impatiently.

Toni lay where she was, looking at him. Her eyes were still dark remembering the most intense emotion she had ever known. Her golden hair fanned out around her head. Her lips were cherry red and swollen from the passion of his kisses.

He leaned over her, one hand on each side of her head. "You are so beautiful, lying there naked with your hair wild about you," he murmured, his voice hoarse. He gave a rough sigh and rested his forehead against hers. "I'd like to say don't move till I get back, my love, but this man is going to paint the house, and he'll probably want to see all of the rooms."

The chimes pealed again and Toni sat up with a start. Her face was crimson.

Nick picked up her clothes and handed them to her as she got to her feet. His hands came down on her shoulders to pull her to him for one more quick hard kiss. "I'll keep him downstairs for a few minutes."

Toni smiled tremulously. "Thanks."

He left the room, and with fumbling fingers she managed to dress. Tidying her hair as best she could with her hands, she slipped out of the room and crept downstairs. She could hear the voices of the two men in the kitchen. She found her purse next to the picnic basket in the parlor. A flick of the comb and a touch of lip gloss restored some of her self-confidence, and when they entered the room a few minutes later, she was curled up in a wing chair beside the crackling fire, flipping idly through a magazine.

8

TONI ARRANGED HER FEATURES into a look of welcoming surprise when the two men entered the room. She was still trembling slightly, and the sight of Nick, tall and virile, had an effect on her that wasn't altogether unexpected. The sudden lurch of her heart, the dryness in her mouth were becoming predictable responses.

"Toni, this is Roy Williams, Aunt Lydia's contractor. Roy, this is the girl I'm going to marry, Miss Grey." Nick watched her tenderly, a small smile on his lips.

Toni froze. Marry! She felt the blood drain from her face, and for a moment thought she would faint. "How...how do you do, Mr. Williams," she managed to say through stiff lips.

"Glad to meet you, Miss Grey." The man evidently didn't notice her reaction. He continued jovially. "I must say, this will be some wedding present, won't it? When we get the kitchen remodeled and fresh paint on the walls, it will really be fine—though Miss Trabert has always kept the place in prime condition," he hastened to add.

"Yes..." Toni said woodenly as she rose to her feet.

"If you'll excuse me, I think I'll wait outside, Nick." Her voice was thick with emotion. She picked up her jacket, clutching it in front of her.

Nick had opened his briefcase on the desk, but at her words he turned, frowning.

"Don't you want to select the colors for the walls, Miss Grey?" Roy Williams asked.

"No!" Toni backed away from Nick's approach.

"Excuse me, Roy. I'll be right back," he said as he took Toni's arm in a firm grip and led her into the hall.

He closed the door behind them and turned her to face him. "What the hell's going on, Toni?"

"Why did you introduce me like that? I'm not your fiancée!" she raved unsteadily.

"You soon will be!"

"No! I can never be that!"

The impact of her words whitened his face. His hands slid up her arms to her shoulders, and he shook her hard. "What are you talking about? Of course you'll marry me!" He was jolted, unbelieving.

"I can't, don't you see that? I can never marry you."

Nick struggled to keep his voice at a low level so as not to be overheard. "Toni, Angela and I made a mistake. I think we both knew it almost from the moment it happened. I can never marry her." His eyes, his voice were pleading.

"Don't marry her then!" Toni cried. "But what we've done is wrong! I won't marry you. Can't you see, Nick? I couldn't live with myself!"

He shook her again, his eyes blazing. "What the hell are you saying? Upstairs, a few minutes ago, I made love to you! Is that any worse? You'd let me do that, but you won't marry me?" His hands tightened on her arms. "I can't believe this!"

Toni threw back her head. "Believe it!" she snapped. Immediately she was sorry for her bluntness, but it was better this way.

He looked at her for a long time. His face slowly turned to stone. There was pain there, and anguish and growing recrimination. Then he pivoted and re-entered the parlor, closing the door behind him with a dull thud.

Pulling on her jacket, Toni walked on rigid legs out the front door and down the steps to the lawn. When she reached the beach she continued down a short flight of wooden steps onto the sand, where she sank down and buried her face in her hands.

When Nick had introduced her as his fiancée, she had been stunned, had suddenly seen herself for what she was. She had behaved disgracefully. How could she and Nick have thought they could have a day out of time? Whatever they took was simply stealing happiness from someone else. What if Angela did love him? How could she live with herself knowing she'd been the cause of their broken engagement? Angela was so loving, so trusting; and she her sister, who should be her closest friend and supporter, had betrayed her instead. Nick's fiancée was still Angela, not Toni. He must have loved her when he asked her to marry him. Even now Toni couldn't help feeling a sudden stab of jealously at the thought of them together.

She groaned and got to her feet, jamming her hands into the pockets of the jacket. The wind had picked up, and it swirled her hair into her face, stinging her eyes. She was cold, so very cold. Looking up at the sky, she began to walk toward the darkening clouds. The waters of the sound were rough now, and the weather matched her mood, gray, bleak, hopeless. *I love him so much*, she cried inside, *and he loves me*. Oh, God! Why couldn't it have been different?

Head bent, she was unaware of his presence until he came up beside her, matching his steps to her shorter ones. He began to talk, not looking at her, but watching their feet move across the sand.

She slid a sideways glance at him, and then quickly looked away.

"I'm thirty-seven years old," he said heavily. His voice was deep and restrained, the anger of a while ago firmly checked. "When I met Angela at a New Year's Eve party this year, I liked her immediately; she's a wonderful girl. We started going out. I knew from the veiled hints Agnes directed at me that she thought Angela should be thinking about marriage. Aunt Lydia has been after me for years to settle down, so I thought, why not? I've known a lot of women, but I had decided that the kind of love my parents had didn't exist for me," he said with harshness. "I think Angela was relieved to have Agnes soothed by an engagement, but both of us have been reluctant all along to set a wedding date. Neither of us, I give you my word, have any illusions about a romantic love between us. I guess we thought love would grow. But then you came home and I was knocked for a loop." He paused and Toni looked at him again.

She immediately regretted it.

His face was pale and drawn, but a glimmer of amusement lit his eyes as he continued. "Both literally and figuratively. Have you always run pell-mell into everything like that?"

Her trembling lips curved into a reluctant smile. "Always. Daddy finally bought me my own pair of crutches. He got tired of renting them."

Nick chuckled. "You need someone to take care of you."

Toni stiffened, clenching her fists. That was the one thing she did not need, that she had worked very hard to make sure she would never need.

Nick looked up at the threatening sky. He hadn't noticed her reaction to his words. "We'd better head back," he said, taking her arm to turn her.

An electric current jolted through her, and she snatched her arm away. "Don't touch me!" she begged.

Again the shuttered look hooded the expression in his eyes, and he rammed his hands back into the pockets of his jeans. There was little enthusiasm in his voice when he said, "I love you. I give you my word, I've never said that to anyone else. I love you and, as a natural extension of that love, I want to marry you. I want us to have a family, to be together forever." His mouth was hard.

The wooden expression was such a contrast to the loving words that Toni had to swallow a hysterical laugh. She realized that this strong-minded man didn't often ask, and he wasn't asking now. She shook her head to clear her eyes. She didn't want to cry. She wouldn't cry! "At the sacrifice of my sister," she choked. "I can't, I can't. It wouldn't work. We could never forget that we took our happiness at the expense of hers."

"Dammit, Toni, I told you! Angela and I have never shared a romantic love! I've never even touched her, kissed her, like I have you!"

Unbidden tears finally spilled from her eyes. He reached for her, but she held him off. "No, no, please. You said 'today!' You said give you today!" She was almost sick. "I can't promise more than that!" She began to back away and Nick stood still, watching her, a thunderous frown crooking his brows.

"You said you love me," he reminded evenly.

"Well, I was wrong!" She denied the truth. "It's a physical attraction. You're very sexy, that's all!" She whirled to run up the beach toward the house.

Blinded by the tears that streamed down her face, Toni lost her sense of direction. When her right foot hit the water she was overcome by shock and fell headfirst into a wave. She was soaked and the waters of the sound were freezing cold. She got awkwardly to her feet and glanced back at Nick. Alarmed, he had started toward her, but she still thought only of flight. She tried to run again, but the cold water had numbed her legs, and she went only a few feet before she fell again. She lay there huddled in misery.

When Nick reached her he bent down and scooped her up. "You little idiot!" he stormed. His long strides covered the distance to the house quickly. He didn't stop when he had her inside but mounted the steps and carried her into the bath off the master suite. "You're crazy! Do you know that? You shouldn't be loose without a keeper!"

She sniffed. "Yes, I know," she said in a subdued voice, but it didn't mollify his anger. She was shivering dangerously by the time he set her on her feet. She watched him turn on the taps in the huge old-fashioned tub resting on clawed feet. Steam rose from the water.

"Get those clothes off!" he ordered as he crossed to a closet door and opened it. He pulled out some towels and threw them onto the padded Victorian bench beside the tub. "Now!"

Her numb fingers fumbled awkwardly with the zipper of the jacket. Nick pushed her hands aside impatiently and unzipped it. He pulled the sodden material off her shoulders and dropped it to the floor. His hands moved to the sweater.

"I...I can do the rest," Toni said hastily.

His black eyes narrowed on her face. "Then do it!"

"When you've left!" She tilted her chin defiantly.

Nick took a deep breath and strode to the door. "I'll wait outside. Hand me the clothes, and I'll take them down to the parlor to dry by the fire," he commanded.

"But I won't have anything to wear!" she protested.

"You certainly can't put those wet things back on. You'd have pneumonia, if you haven't already!" He raked his hair with an irritated hand. "I'll try to find you something!"

When he stepped outside, she quickly stripped the clothes from her body and, from behind the protection of the door, handed the wet bundle to him. She hesitated before closing the door. Through chattering teeth she murmured, "Thank you, Nick."

"Don't thank me. I'd do the same for any drowned rat! Hurry up and get into that bath!"

She obeyed and sank down into the warm water, her thoughts desolate. She was intelligent, capable, self-sufficient... until a tall dark devil had come into her life, turning her into a mass of quivering jelly. He was probably glad now that she'd refused to marry him. She bit back a sob. What else could she do? She'd stolen her sister's fiancé. That's what it came down to. But could she live without him? It was a question for which she had no answer.

The water began to cool, and she added some more hot to it. Her tears mingled with the water when she dipped under the surface to rinse the salt from her hair.

As soon as she stepped from the tub the chill in the air started her shivering again. She wrapped one towel around her hair and tucked another one across her breasts. A third was draped over her shoulders. On freezing feet she tiptoed to the door.

Nick stood at the window, hands pushed into his pockets, looking out at the rain that had begun to fall with a brooding expression. His strong profile was visible in the reflection of the glass, and he must have caught her movement there because he turned.

He took in her shivering form, from the bare legs and feet, to the turban around her head. He picked up something from a chair and handed it to her. "I always carry an extra dress shirt in my briefcase. It's all I could find for you to wear."

She nodded and closed the door between them. Draping the towels cross the edge of the tub, she quickly put the shirt on. She looked at herself in the full-length mirror in one corner. The tails of the shirt, front and back, came to her knees, but the sides revealed more thigh than she would have liked. The cuffs hid her hands, so she rolled them back twice to her wrists. Nick must have very long arms.... The thought caused a quickening of her heartbeat. Slowly she ran her hands up her arms, crossing them in front of her to hug her shoulders. Wherever the material touched, she was warm. The soft cotton enfolded her like an embrace. She closed her eyes for a moment, relishing the brush of his shirt against her skin. Oh, God! This would never do! She started to unbutton it but stopped. She had nothing else to wear.

When Toni reentered the bedroom Nick was standing there with a blanket in his hands. At the sight of her he gripped the material until his knuckles were white. His eyes darkened to a gleaming onyx as he took a sharp breath.

Toni studied the floor in front of her. "It...it's a little too big," she murmured, unable to meet his eyes.

Nick looked at her bent head, heavy with the white towel turban and let the air out of his lungs slowly. "Yes, well, it's the best I could do," he said harshly.

Her eyes lifted. "Oh, I didn't mean that! To complain, I mean...."

He shrugged at the disjointed phrases. "I know what you mean. Are your feet cold?"

She looked down and wiggled her toes, curling them under. "They are freezing." She stood perfectly still as he moved forward to wrap the wool blanket around her. When he picked her up in his arms she almost gave in to the urge to rest her head against the broad shoulder. An almost imperceptible shudder went through her at his touch, even through the heavy blanket.

"At least the parlor's warm," he said as he started out of the room.

Had he felt the shudder? He must have, and thought her reaction was to the cold. It was just as well.

"I'm sorry, Nick. It was a stupid thing to do," she admitted ruefully.

"Which stupid thing do you mean, Toni?" he asked blandly. "You seem to do quite a few."

She caught her lip between her teeth. "I deserved that, I guess."

"That and more!" Nick said. Her carried her effortlessly down the stairs.

"Well, I've apologized!" she said defensively as he set her on her feet in front of the fire.

"Yes! You've apologized!" He gripped her shoulders roughly. "In your own irrational senseless way. What a lawyer you're going to make!" He was almost shouting.

"You alternate between absolute fury and concern, and call me irrational?" she shouted back.

"Sit down and shut up if you don't want to see just how furious I can be!"

Nick had transferred the cushions from the sofa and arranged them in front of the fire. When he folded the fire screen back, Toni felt the warmth of the glaze invade her stiff limbs. She trembled, undecided as to whether she should answer him back. Finally she gave up and sank onto the cushions. Nick sat beside her and moved her feet across his lap. Unwrapping the blanket from around them, his big hands began to massage the feeling back. He worked on one foot and then the other. With the return of feeling came a tingling pain.

"Ouch! That hurts!" She tried to pull them away, but he held on.

"It will stop hurting in a minute. You've got to get your circulation going." He resumed the deft rubbing.

"You don't have to try to be nice to me, since I realize it's an effort!"

Nick's blazing eyes turned on her. "You're damned right it's an effort! But we can't leave here until your clothes are dry, so we may as well be civil!"

Toni gasped at the antagonistic look in his eyes and tried to be calm, sitting quietly as he massaged her feet. He said he loved her. He couldn't love her very much and treat her like this! No one had ever shouted at her before, she thought unhappily. Not even Agnes. She made her displeasure known by a cold expression, but she didn't shout.

"I'm sure you're breathing a sigh of relief that I can't marry you," Toni said, wincing inwardly at the wound she was inflicting on herself.

He looked at her sharply but didn't answer.

"After all, with the life you lead you need someone who can entertain gracefully," she persisted. "Someone charming, like Angela, who never had a broken bone or a sprained ankle."

The muscle in his jaw jerked.

"A well-organized hostess."

"Shut up, Toni!" he ground out between clenched teeth. "If I'd wanted a hostess, I'd have arranged for one. I wanted a woman, mature enough to accept responsibility. What I found was an intelligent child, posing as a woman, who wanted the satisfaction of the moment, but no commitment."

Toni lifted her chin. "You don't understand."

"That's the age-old pleading of a child! You're the one who doesn't understand," he said harshly. "Life isn't like that, Toni. Not black and white, right and wrong! You have to try to negotiate, to give a little and take a little. Sometimes we make mistakes. We're only human. But then we have to make an effort to rectify them, carefully, trying to leave as little destruction as possible.''

Toni started to say something else, then firmly closed her mouth. It would be better if they didn't discuss it further. He wasn't going to try to understand her point of view, and she wouldn't change her mind. She watched him in the firelight. Although it was early afternoon, the rain had darkened the day to twilight. The golden glow from the flames bathed the strong masculine planes of his face. Her eyes lingered on the sensual mouth, the powerful neck and the sturdy chest. A few thick curling hairs were visible above the button of his shirt. The warm heavy feeling was beginning again in the pit of her stomach. Her heart began to skip its steady rhythm at the touch of his hands. She wished he would stop. She swallowed to bring moisture to her dry throat and tugged her feet, trying to move away.

Nick's hands stilled as his gaze locked with hers. One hand left the sole of the foot he was holding and moved to the ankle. The massage gentled as his fingers slid up to stroke the inside of her calf and around to the back of her knee. He watched her reaction with an expression of satisfaction.

She couldn't tear her eyes from his unrelenting gaze.

Finally he broke off the silent communication and wrapped her feet back in their warm cocoon before swinging them off his lap. He stood up. "Are you hungry?" he asked casually, crossing to lift the picnic basket.

Toni couldn't answer. The muscles in his shoulders bunched under the shirt, and she longed to caress them.

"Silly question. Of course you are." His voice dropped an octave, and his eyes were veiled by long lashes as he settled back down on the cushion. There was a hint of a knowing masculine smile on his face. He was playing with her, as a cat plays with a mouse before moving in for the kill. He knew what effect his touch, the warmth of the fire and the dim flickering light were having on her. He was a master in the art of seduction, and if she weren't careful she would be a willing pupil.

Toni struggled to sit up and free her arms and hands. She pretended to ignore his suggestive statement. "Yes, I'm starving." She arranged the blanket around her waist securely. If he could be cold and unrelenting, so could she. At least, she could try.

"Okay. Let's see what we have." He put the basket between them and flipped back the lid. A bottle of red wine rested on the top, and he lifted it off. "Ah, a Burgundy. Excellent. We'll let it breathe while we eat." He rummaged round in the basket and came up with a corkscrew. "See what else Jane packed for us," he said as he pulled the seal away from the cork.

Toni lifted the corner of a red-and-white checked tablecloth and took out several foil-wrapped packages and a thermos. Her hands were both full. She tried to nudge the basket out of the way with her knee, but that dislodged the blanket and one bare leg was uncovered. Her eyes flew to him.

"Having trouble?" he asked smoothly.

"Yes," she answered shortly.

He moved the basket away, then spread the cloth on the cushion between them.

Toni dumped the packages on the cloth and quickly pulled the blanket back around her legs.

Nick finally had the cork free, and he set the bottle of wine on the floor behind them, away from the fire.

The packages revealed thick roast-beef sandwiches, tiny tomatoes stuffed with a cream-cheese mixture, deviled eggs and delicate cream puffs. A wedge of Brie cheese and two plump ripe peaches were still in the basket.

"Good heavens! This is enough for an army!" Toni laughed nervously. She was unbalanced by his alertness, and the strange smile he wore.

"It may have to be enough for dinner, too, if your clothes don't get dry."

She looked at him surprised. "Where are they?"

"Behind you."

She twisted around to see her clothes draped over a chair angled toward the fire. Her lacy bra and panties were artistically arranged on the seat. She blushed furiously and refused to meet his eyes.

"I've seen them before."

Toni lifted her chin. "I know you have," she said with studied indifference. She unscrewed the top from the thermos. "Would you like some coffee?"

There was a hint of devilment in his eye. "Yes. You'd better have some, too, to warm you up."

Toni watched him warily and reached for a sandwich. As they ate she began to relax. Occasionally they spoke quietly.

After their hunger had been assuaged, Nick reached for his coffee. "Jane never disappoints me. Wait till you taste her cream puffs. They're as light as a feather."

Toni bit into one with her sharp white teeth. "Mmm, they are good!" A bit of custard filling clung to her lip, and she caught it with her tongue.

Nick's eyes darkened as they followed the movement and lingered on her lips. "Are you insane or just naive?" he rasped.

"What?" She was startled out of her comfortable mood, and frowned.

"Forget it!" He started rewrapping the food and returned the packages to the basket. "Would you like some wine and cheese?"

"Maybe later," she answered, subdued.

When the food was packed away Nick poured himself a glass of wine and leaned back on an elbow. His head was almost touching her arm, but he paid no attention, staring into the fire.

Toni wasn't as successful as he was in ignoring their proximity. Aware of that dark head, she longed to run her fingers through the thick hair at his nape. When he tilted the glass up she was hypnotized by the muscles in his throat. Again she felt her passion rise. She fought to cool it, but her pulse began to race.

This situation was becoming impossible! Though they sat here conversing on one level like conventional adults, there was another level of communication, an underlying torment of need and longing that had Toni yearning for his touch.

Suddenly he leaned his head back and looked up at her. She thought if he took her in his arms now there wouldn't be a thing she could do to stop him. She didn't have the will to protest and he knew it. She realized from his complacent expression that he was reading her thought precisely.

He lifted his arm and she held her breath. But his hand went to the damp towel still wrapped around her head. "We need to get your hair dry." He sat up.

Toni gave a half-hysterical laugh.

"What's funny?"

"Nothing! Nothing. You're right." She reached up and pulled the towel off. Leaning forward, she began to rub her hair vigorously with the towel. The curtain of hair over her face hid her expression, until he put down his wineglass and took the towel away.

"That won't work. The towel's wet. Turn around." He turned her shoulders and pulled her around until her head was across his lap, where her feet had been. He reached under her neck and fanned the hair out. "It will dry faster this way."

Toni looked up at him, but he was watching his fingers comb through the tawny mass.

He lifted a strand and let it fall. He lifted another. Bringing it forward, he brushed it slowly down her cheek and across her lips. When he lowered himself onto his elbow this time, his face was over hers, but he didn't meet her wide-eyed gaze. He was engrossed in tracing each feature with his brush of hair, up the bridge of her nose to her forehead and across her eyes. Her lids fell, then opened again when she felt the brush on her chin. He traced down her throat to where the buttons of his shirt joined and back up to her lips. Dropping the hair, he took up where he left off with his fingers stroking, teasing.

"Are you trying to seduce me?" Toni asked huskily. She felt weak, boneless.

He looked into her eyes and smiled, then his attention returned to her lips. "If I were, would it work?" he asked softly. He leaned forward and outlined her lips with his tongue.

"I...I'm not sure, but..." He took advantage of her parted lips to invade her mouth. His tongue slid over her teeth and caressed the underside of her upper lip.

Toni groaned mindlessly and tried to deepen the kiss, but Nick pulled back. He took her by the shoulders and sat her up, facing him.

His long legs stretched behind her. Sinking back onto his elbow, he let his hand rove over her shoulder and up to her neck. "Do you like wearing my shirt?" he asked as his fingers wandered down to the V between her breasts.

"Hmm?" She hardly knew what he was saying. She just wanted this delicious caressing to go on and on.

He loosened a button, then another. His fingers

slipped in to brush the curve of her breast. "Do you like the way my shirt feels against your naked skin?" he murmured hypnotically.

"Yes, yes, I do," she whispered.

His fingers ventured further and touched a hardening nipple.

Her body's response was instantaneous. She moaned, "Nick, what are you doing to me?"

Quickly he released the rest of the buttons down to where the blanket protected the lower half of her body. He pulled the shirt open and cupped a breast in his palm.

She was barely breathing. As his hand stroked, massaged, a ball of tension was building in her midriff.

His lips joined his hand on her sensitive skin. "Do you want me to make love to you, Toni?" he whispered against the tender curve of her breast.

Her fingers raked through his hair. Her eyes were closed, her head had fallen back. She was once again lost in the whirlwind of feelings. "Oh, yes, I do. Please. Nick, I want you," she answered thickly.

He raised himself until his lips hovered over hers. "I want you, darling. And I'll make love to you." He tasted her lips. "Just as soon as you agree to marry me."

She lifted her arms to bring his lips back to her. "What?"

He kissed her again, deeply, and pulled back to look at her face with absolute seriousness. "I said I'll make love to you, as soon as you agree to marry me."

Toni opened her heavy eyes. What was he talking about? "Nick?"

Her eyes widened, as his meaning dawned on her. "You mean...? You did this to me...to...."

"I'll do anything I have to to force a commitment from you," he replied. His hands were on her shoulders. "Anything!"

She shook her head, unable to understand. "How could you?" she accused. "That's a horrible thing to do!"

"Are you going to marry me?"

"I can't," she murmured. "Nick, I can't! Please try to see my side. Listen, I—"

"No!" he interrupted. "I can't take any of your crazy brand of logic at the moment!" he thrust her away and got to his feet. "I'm going for a walk!" He grabbed his jacket and headed for the door.

"In the rain? You can't!" she cried. "Nick, be reasonable!"

He pivoted, slinging down the jacket and towering over her. His anger was a frightening thing and she cringed.

"I've tried to reason with you. It doesn't work! Who the hell do you think you are to set yourself up as judge and jury on the happiness of others. Angela will be better off without me, since I don't love her." He paced furiously away from her and back again. "You gave up your close relationship with your father to make Agnes happy. You're giving me up to make Angela happy. Well, what about my happiness? How are you going to arrange that Miss Fix-it?

Or don't my feelings matter to you at all?'' Rage was building in him.

''Yes! You know they do!'' she said, agonized.

''Only enough to let me make love to you again!'' he said sarcastically. ''You'd have let me do that! You wouldn't have been able to live with yourself afterward, but you'd have let me.''

Toni bowed her head under his tirade.

''On the other hand why should you get any pleasure out of it?'' He was on his knees beside her. ''I might as well take what has been so blatantly offered to me. God knows, I want you badly enough. At least then I won't have to take a cold shower.'' He grabbed an edge of the blanket and yanked it violently, rolling her out onto the floor.

''Nick, no!''

''Nick, yes! That's what you've been saying to me ever since we got here! How much do you expect me to take of this?'' With shaking hands he jerked the shirt apart, taking the last button off, and looked at her hungrily. Then he pulled her into his arms and his mouth crushed hers.

Toni pushed against his chest.

His hands moved over her roughly. He lifted her onto the cushions and as he stood up, unbuttoning his shirt, his eyes burned over her body. The shirt fell to the floor, and his hands went to the buckle of his belt.

Toni's eyes widened in alarm. She rolled away, trying to get to her feet, but he grabbed her and brought her back.

He came down on top of her, one leg pinning hers, his hand in her hair to hold her head still while his hard mouth tormented hers.

Toni lay trembling under his rough hands. "Not like this, Nick. You don't want this!" she cried.

"Don't I? Maybe you'll get pregnant and have to marry me!" He laughed unpleasantly. Gripping her chin in iron fingers, his hostile mouth once more invaded hers.

Despite his anger, which Toni knew she had brought on, she felt herself responding to the appeal of his lips. The male smell of him was intoxicating. But she had to stop this trespass on her body. Neither of them would ever forget if he took her this way. She wrenched her mouth away and said hoarsely, "There's always abortion."

Nick froze. He looked at her with eyes that held a haunting mixture of fury and despair.

Toni looked at him and wished she could have bitten off her tongue before saying the words that put that grimace on his face.

"Would you do that?" he finally asked.

"No! No, I wouldn't! I'm sorry. That was a rotten thing to say. Please forgive me," she begged. "You frightened me, and I. . . . But I should never have said it."

Nick's eyes moved over her features as though he couldn't believe his eyes. He raised an unsteady hand to touch her wet face, her softly swollen lips. He shuddered convulsively and buried his face in her neck. "God, Toni! What am I doing to you?" He looked at her again, his eyes bright with moisture. Slowly he released her. Pulling the side of the shirt together, he settled her back on the cushions and got to his feet. He looked dazed. "My God! What's happened to me? I used to be a half-civilized man!" he groaned, his face distorted. He leaned down to pick up his shirt and jacket.

Toni sat up, alarmed. "Where are you going?"

"Out!" He headed unsteadily toward the door.

"In the rain?" she persisted, getting to her knees. She put up a hand to push her hair back. The other hand gripped the sides of the shirt together.

"I'll take the car."

"Nick, please don't drive like this." She was really frightened for him now.

"Toni," he warned threateningly, "don't say any more!" He stopped. "I'll be back for you." Then he opened the door.

Toni looked at his back, but she didn't say anything else.

Before he closed the door he turned to look at her, kneeling in the firelight, her hair in wild disorder, her face blotched from crying and her lips swollen. His hand tightened on the knob. "I'll be back for you," he repeated. "Cover up with the blanket. I don't want you to catch cold." He left.

TONI DIDN'T HEAR NICK when he returned two hours later. She was upstairs in the bathroom splashing cold water on her face in a futile attempt to erase the signs of her recent tears. Her jeans had finally dried and so had her nylon jacket, but the wool sweater was still wet, so she kept on Nick's shirt. The tails were stuffed down into her jeans. She retrieved her purse from the bedroom and took out her comb and lipstick.

Five minutes later she surveyed the wreck in the mirror. It was no use. She looked terrible. Shrugging, she descended the steps on bare feet. Her sneakers weren't dry yet.

At the door to the parlor she stopped.

Nick sat in a chair, his elbows resting on his knees, staring down at her sweater in his clenched fists.

As she watched he groaned and buried his face in the blue material.

She moved forward and touched him on the shoulder. "Nick."

He jumped as though he had been shot and looked up at her. He got to his feet and grasped her shoulders. "I thought you had left." His voice was hoarse.

"No, I was upstairs," she explained softly.

He groaned again and wrapped his arms, warm and tight, around her.

Toni melted against him for a moment, only to be held suddenly at arm's length.

"I'm sorry, Toni." He turned away and rammed his hand into his pockets. "I promised myself I wouldn't touch you again."

"But, Nick...." She shook her head helplessly. He was right, she knew that; but unreasonably, .he thought of never again feeling those muscular arms around her was unbearable.

He interrupted impatiently. "No, Toni! Forget it. Forget me!" His breathing was labored. "I've been driving around. Thinking. And I've decided you're right. It just wouldn't work. What we feel for each other is probably forbidden appeal. I give you my word I won't bother you again!"

"And Angela?" Toni couldn't prevent the question from popping out.

"I'm not going to marry her, Toni, but don't blame yourself. It was already an unlikely event." He picked up the picnic basket and his briefcase and looked around the room. "Let's go."

Toni looked around, too. This room had been heaven and hell for her, and she would never forget it. She had returned the cushions to the sofa and replaced the screen in front of the cold fire. All at once she felt as cold and dead as the ashes. Tears again filled her blue eyes. She turned away quickly, but Nick had seen.

"For God's sake, don't cry! I don't think I can stand it," he said roughly.

"I'm sorry." Toni straightened her shoulders. "I don't ever cry." She started to the door. "Don't worry about me, Nick. I'll be all right." *Maybe... someday*, she added to herself.

"Yes, I'm sure you will," he answered heavily.

9

It was a week later to the day. Toni pulled off her Sunday-afternoon uniform, a dark blue warm-up suit. She tried to exercise every Sunday, to stretch the muscles that were stiff and tight from sitting all week. The brisk walk through the gardens and a brief run along the river's edge had helped clear her mind as well as loosen her muscles. She stepped into the shower and stood with her back to the pulsating spray, letting it finish the job with a soft massage of water. Fifteen minutes later she was ready to leave.

She decided not to bother taking her car to the hospital. The Boston Medical Center was on the subway line, and it was always such a chore to search for a parking space. She pulled on a white wool blazer over a peach sweater and matching slacks and gave her reflection a last check in the mirror before leaving the apartment. Too pale! Impatiently she reached for a compact of blush. The soft sable brush skimmed over her cheeks, leaving just a hint of color.

Suddenly the brush slipped from her nerveless fingers and fell to the floor. The sensation had brought it all back. She could almost feel Nick's brush of hair tracing her features, see the forceful intelligent planes in his face bathed in firelight. As she reached down to pick up her brush, she could also see a silent steel-jawed Nick as he let her out in front of her apartment building later that night.

Angela had called the next afternoon to tell her that the engagement was off. Nick certainly hadn't wasted any time. One part of Toni's heart had leaped at the news, but the other had still thumped heavily with its burden of guilt.

It had been a strange conversation, Angela sounding more distracted than depressed. Or was that only wishful thinking?

"Are you all right, Angela?" she'd asked tentatively. Her palms were suddenly clammy. She rubbed one against the leg of her jeans and shifted the receiver to repeat the action with the other hand.

"I'm fine," answered her sister. "At least I think, I am," she added softly. "Or I will be if—" She broke off. "This at least solves the problem of us being there for your graduation." She sounded determinedly cheerful. "What shall I wear?"

Toni had laughed. It was so typical of her sister to worry first about her wardrobe. "A ball gown and diamonds!" she teased unsteadily.

Angela giggled. "I'm serious, Toni. What *does* one wear to graduation at the world's most prestigious law school?"

"I have no idea. I've never been, myself, but you'll look gorgeous in anything," she assured her sister.

The conversation had finally dwindled. When Toni hung up it was with an overwhelming feeling of relief.

Nick had evidently left her name out of it completely, and why not? She had taken herself out with the denial of her love and her refusal to marry him. What else could she have done? She almost cried the words aloud.

She had tried at first to tell herself that the entire weekend was a bubble out of time, separated from reality by thin translucent walls, but nevertheless separated. It was not a part of her real life and, as such, was nothing she could be judged on. When she reexamined that idea she was horrified. It was a measure of her despair that she would try to justify her actions without accepting responsibility for them.

The intervening week had been the most miserable she'd ever spent, but ironically it had also been good for her. It had forced her to take a hard look at herself and to answer some of the questions Nick had raised. Was she afraid of commitment? She had labored for seven long years to attain the goal of a meaningful career and in the process had put her emotions on a back burner. Now they clamored for attention.

On Wednesday she'd had another call from Atlanta. In a cold indifferent voice Nick informed her that Nervy would be arriving today to check into the Boston Medical Center. The tests would begin Monday.

She'd had to take a breath to calm her throbbing pulse before she could answer. "What time does her plane arrive, Nick? I'll meet her."

He hesitated. "Douglas and I will be with her. Perhaps it would be better if you see her when she's settled into the hospital."

"Of course," she answered quietly, inwardly raging at him. Who was he to make all these arrangements that excluded her?

"Douglas is staying at Aunt Lydia's, Toni," he explained evenly. "I'm just coming along to make him feel comfortable."

"Certainly, Nick. I understand," she said in a brittle tone.

He gave an impatient hiss. "Toni—"

"Thank you for calling, Nick. Goodbye." She hung up quickly before he could recognize her true emotions from her voice.

The next day Toni had left the campus after her last class and headed directly for a building she had noticed one day while driving past. She maneuvered her car into a parking spot under the red, white and blue sign, which read Travel Agents International. Nick's words echoed in her brain as she climbed out of the car. "You can't go on that trip alone, you know." Well, she *would* go on the trip alone. She could take care of herself very well. She didn't need anyone.

A neat pleasant woman in a crisp blue blazer was alone in the office. She looked up from a computer console. "May I help you?" she asked.

"Yes," Toni answered decisively. "I would like to book a flight to Rome, Italy." She had decided last night after poring over the atlas that Rome would be a good jumping-off place for her trip.

"Of course. We'll be happy to do that for you. When would you like to go?"

"Any time after the first week in June," Toni responded.

"And will you want a round-trip ticket or one way?"

The woman smiled, and suddenly Toni realized that she wasn't well prepared for this conversation at all. Her thoughts had been focused on escape and escape only. She hadn't considered what she would do when it was time to come home, or where she would be. "Perhaps I should come back later," she offered with a rueful grin.

The woman took in her hesitation and got to her feet. She unlatched a portion of the counter, lifting it for Toni to pass through. "Why don't you have a seat here," she said, indicating a chair beside her desk. "I'll get us some coffee and you can tell me what you've planned." Her brows lifted. "Or haven't planned?"

An hour later Toni emerged from the building, her hands filled with colorful brochures and her mind whirling with thoughts of passports, visas, international drivers' licenses and fares. She had made a sincere promise to return tomorrow better informed. Judy, the agent, assured her that it wasn't as complicated as it looked, but she also warned that some of the visas could take several weeks to obtain even if they were rushed. "If you really want to leave in June we need to get the applications in immediately.

"Thanks a lot, Judy. You've been very patient," Toni had told her sincerely.

"That's my job, Toni." She waved as Toni left.

When she got to her apartment she fixed a quick supper and spread the brochures around her on the table as she ate. The views were beautiful and the descriptions exciting, but was this really what she wanted? As she munched on her sandwich she wondered if the pain would be any less halfway around the world than it was here.

She still hadn't decided when she pushed open the glass door of the travel office the next afternoon. There were several customers today. Two couples were talking to a man in a blazer, the emblem on his pocket the same as the one Judy sported. Judy herself was smiling at an elderly woman as she handed over a ticket envelope. "Have a nice trip, Mrs. Ray. Be sure to bring us back a picture of the grandchildren."

The woman beamed at the thoughtful request. "I will, Judy. Goodbye."

"Hi, Judy." Toni smiled and held up her international driver's license.

"Toni! You've been busy," Judy remarked approvingly.

"It was as easy as you said it would be. I've had my pictures made for the passport, wrote for a copy of my birth certificate, and . . . what else?" She frowned. "Darn! I'm sure there was something else." Her brow cleared. "Oh, yes. I've brought my checkbook."

"Good!" Judy rubbed her hands togeher. "Now we can get started."

Toni had decided to stay for two months. As she wrote out the check for the round-trip airline fare, she felt peculiarly light-headed. A decision had been reached and there was no going back. A picture of Nick flashed before her, and she closed her eyes momentarily against the pain. Time, that was what she needed, time and distance. She would get over this. No one died of a broken heart. She was healthy, had a promising career ahead of her. She would get over it. But her hand faltered on her signature.

Judy was a sharp-eyed lady. "It isn't irreversible, you know. We can always cancel," she said quietly.

"I don't know what you mean," Toni answered evenly. She raised blank eyes to meet Judy's, hoping that her expression wouldn't reflect how lost she felt.

Judy watched her for a long minute. Finally she took a breath. "Then let me explain. I sell tickets for all kinds of journeys. Vacations, honeymoons, business trips." She paused and her voice warmed as she said with a soft smile, "Trips to visit families like Mrs. Ray's. She's so excited about those grandchildren out in Oregon. Other family trips aren't so happy, when you have to fly to the side of a loved one who is ill." Shaking her head, she continued, "Anyway, I've gotten rather good at guessing what kind of trip my clients are taking even if they don't tell me. My radar senses that this isn't a vacation for you. You're running away from something or someone. Right?" she asked gently.

Toni marveled at her insight even while she deplored it, but she couldn't think of a reason to evade the question. She shrugged her slender shoulders and smiled sadly. "Right."

"Are you sure you have to run?" Judy persisted, still in that same gentle tone. "Most things look very black up close, but with a little perspective—"

Toni interrupted her. "Thanks, Judy. I appreciate your concern. But that's just what I'm giving myself, a little perspective." She reached for her purse with a gesture of decisiveness and got to her feet. "I'll let you know about the hotel reservations and the car rental, okay?"

"Okay." Judy looked as though she'd failed at something that was important to her. "If you say so."

"I do. I'll call you soon. Bye."

"Bye, Toni."

"And, Judy, I meant it when I said thanks."

The two couples were still in earnest conversation with the other agent when she let herself out. She walked with a more confident step toward her car. There were a lot of good caring people in this world, she thought, and she'd just been lucky enough to meet one of them.

NOW SHE LOOKED AROUND distractedly for her purse. She had checked with the hospital. Mrs. Minerva Davis was in Room 432 and visiting hours began at seven. Douglas would surely be there. Would Nick? She didn't think she could bear trying to make small talk with him. She left the apartment and walked the few blocks to the subway entrance, stopping on her way to buy a bouquet of spring blossoms.

Nervy was tense and anxious. Douglas sat in an

upright chair beside the bed, holding tightly to her hand.

Toni standing at the door to her room, was shocked by her appearance. Her cheeks were hollow and she looked tired. The thick hair with its streaks of gray looked dull and lifeless against the white pillow. Toni smothered a gasp and put on a determined smile before she pushed farther into the room. "Welcome to Boston!"

Two pairs of frightened eyes turned to her. Nervy's warmed instantly. "Toni, child! I'm so glad to see you. What beautiful flowers!"

Toni leaned down to kiss the weathered cheek and smooth the gray hair. Her voice stuck somewhere in her throat, but when she saw Nervy's eyes fill with tears she swallowed her own. "I'm glad to see both of you, too, but not like this. You haven't been taking care of yourself, Nervy," she scolded gently. Nervy's sharp eyes roamed knowingly over Toni's slim form. "You don't look too well yourself, child. You've lost weight, haven't you?"

Toni squirmed under the appraisal. "Yes, a little," she answered in what she hoped was an offhand way. "I've been working hard."

"I know. Nick told us."

Her eyes met Nervy's in surprise. "He did?"

Nervy watched the slow flush creep up her face. "Yes, he said that these last few weeks of school were going to be very difficult for you. He's been wonderful to us, Toni. You know that Douglas is staying with Nick's aunt?"

"Yes. I've met her. She's an admirable woman, isn't she?"

"Very admirable and very kind," Douglas interjected.

"Douglas, would you mind asking the nurse for something cool to drink? I'm thirsty." Nervy smiled at him.

"Sure, Minerva. I'll get a vase for the flowers, too." He went out.

Nervy waited until the door had closed behind him before she said, "Nick had no reason to be so concerned about me anymore, Toni. Did you know that Nick and Angela are no longer engaged?"

Toni fought the constriction in her chest and decided that there was no point in trying to deceive her old nurse. "Yes, Angela called me. But Nick wouldn't let that stop him, Nervy. He likes you."

The older woman observed her reaction with a marked scrutiny. "Well, I'm grateful. He is a fine man. I'm just sorry he won't be in the family."

Toni avoided her eyes. "I guess Agnes is upset."

"Mrs. Grey is fit to be tied." Nervy agreed, still watching. "She's told all of her friends that Nick deceived that sweet child."

Oh, no! Toni groaned inwardly. "Poor Angela!" she said aloud. She got to her feet, moving restlessly around the room.

"Poor Angela, my foot! She should be glad! I can't imagine anything worse than marrying someone you don't love fully and completely. It's 'poor Nick' as far as I'm concerned," she said firmly. "He looks terrible—'' She broke off what she'd been about to say when a nurse came in with thermometer and blood-pressure cuff.

Toni had to bite her lip to keep from demanding that Nervy finish her sentence. Nick looked terribly what? Finally the white-clad woman bustled out again, but Nervy didn't pick up the conversation where she'd broken off. Instead she said bluntly, ''Toni, I'm going to ask you something, and I don't want you to lie to me.''

Toni approached the bed wearing a half-smile and cocked her head. ''I've never lied to you Nervy,'' she said softly.

Nervy returned the smile with satisfaction. ''I know.'' She took a breath. ''Toni, something happened last weekend. I don't want to know what it was. All I want to know is this—do you love Nick?''

Toni didn't look at her. ''Yes,'' she said with no attempt at equivocation. It wouldn't have done any good anyway, but that one word was one of the most difficult she'd ever spoken. Would she see disgust in Nervy's eyes? She summoned the courage to look, and what she read made her sink into the chair in stunned surprise.

An even wider smile curved Nervy's thin lips. ''Good!'' she said.

''There's nothing good about it!'' Toni said with spirit.

''Yes, there is, honey. He loves you, too. I think that he'll ask you to marry him.''

Toni got to her feet again and began to pace. ''He already has, Nervy. I turned him down.''

Nervy didn't speak and Toni went on quickly, trying to explain. "We could never be happy."

"Because of Angela? Pooh!" Nervy said, dismissing with a wave of her hand all of the unspoken objections. "You'd better jump at the chance if he asks you again!"

Toni had to smile. Nervy made it sound so simple. "I doubt he will do that," she said sadly. "I think I did a pretty good job of convincing him that I didn't love him."

"Then you'll have to ask him!"

Toni looked at her for a moment without seeing. Ask him?

"Toni, Nick Trabert is worth fighting for!" Nervy urged strongly.

Could she? What would she be opening herself up to if he refused? More humiliation and heartache? But then, could she possibly hurt more than she had for the past week?

Before she could take the thought any further Douglas reentered the room with a glass of juice and a large green vase.

Toni took the vase and filled it with water from the small sink.

"This is all you can have tonight," Douglas said to his wife. "The tests begin in the morning." He smiled down at her. "And the nurse gave me a gentle hint to leave soon. She said they want you to have a good night's sleep."

Toni finished arranging the flowers and left the couple to say their goodbyes, promising to return the following night.

As she stood at the door, Nervy gave one last parting shot. "Have I ever given you bad advice, child? You think over what I've said."

"Yes. Yes, Nervy, I will." She certainly would think it over. She had missed him so. Could she live with herself if she didn't try? For the first time, Toni forced herself to look objectively at the doubts Angela had made plain in their telephone conversation. Had she been a fool? So convinced was she that the attraction she felt for Nick was wrong that she'd refused to examine her sister's words and actions. But Nervy had. Their nurse knew the girls better than they knew themselves.

As she descended the steps at the front of the hospital, she was obeying Nervy's directive to the exclusion of everything else. Perhaps that was why it was both a shock and an inevitability to see the object of her thoughts, standing in her path, hands thrust into the pockets of a pair of jeans.

Nick's face was partly in shadow, but she could see that his cheeks were leaner, his mouth harder. He watched her with hooded eyes as she approached slowly on trembling legs. "Hello, Toni," he said formally. His face was impassive.

The sound of the deep voice shook her even more than she thought it would. She wanted to hurl herself into his strong arms, feel them close around her and stay there forever. Instead she forced a serenity into her voice that she didn't feel and greeted him calmly. "Hello, Nick."

"How are you?" Her shiver was only partly the

result of the chill of the night air. She took a deep breath. "Are you waiting for Douglas?"

"Yes."

"He shouldn't be long. The nurses want to make sure Nervy gets a good night's sleep."

"I'm in no hurry."

Toni started to say something. She wasn't sure what the words would have been, but she couldn't get them out anyway in the face of this cold hostility. "Well...goodnight." She let her hair, worn loose tonight, swing forward to hide her eyes from him and moved away.

"Where's your car?" He turned to walk beside her. His long legs took one step to her two.

"I didn't want to bother parking it. I took the subway," she said, increasing her pace.

But Nick wasn't to be avoided. His hand caught her elbow.

The contact was like a jolt of electricity through them both. In the light from a streetlamp she could see him whiten, and she was sure that her own face mirrored his shock.

Annoyed at his reaction, Nick dropped his hand, recovering quickly. Still she thought she discerned a slight huskiness in his voice when he spoke. "I'll take you home."

She was wary of his withdrawn courtesy, but was the self-control an act? Could Nick possibly be as miserable as she was? "That isn't necessary," she told him quietly.

"I know that! You made it quite plain last weekend, Toni, that you don't need anyone!" The cool demeanor cracked. "Just say I'll feel better. Okay?" he demanded angrily.

"No, it is not okay!" The taut strand that was her own composure suddenly snapped. "I've been riding on these subways for seven years, and I've never even been propositioned!"

"The muggers were probably afraid of ice burn," he muttered under his breath.

"Wha-a-t?" Her voice rose. She knew she hadn't misunderstood. The anger she had felt at his high-handed attitude multiplied with the insult. She whirled and started to stalk off.

Nick caught her elbow again. "I'm sorry, Toni. I shouldn't have said that."

He didn't sound sorry. She pulled against his hold. "It's all right. Just let me go."

"I can't." His voice was suddenly husky and her eyes flew up to meet his. "I mean...please, let me take you home."

She searched his face, but his expression told her nothing. "All right," she finally murmured.

There didn't seem to be any more to say. Toni slid her hands into the pockets of her jacket and took a meandering step or two. The silence between them was heavy. Toni felt its sad weight on her shoulders. If she stretched out a hand she could touch the man she loved, but the barrier was more substantial than mere air. Nervy was wrong.

"Have you decided yet what you're going to do after graduation?"

She risked a glance to find him watching her. "No, I—er...well, not about a job." You finally managed to finish the sentence, she told herself in disgust. This was unbearable. She shouldn't have let him talk her into waiting. Where *was* Douglas anyway?

"What, then?" Nick pressed.

Her chin came up. She might as well tell him. "I've decided to take that trip to the Middle East," she said.

His temper erupted, just as she had expected. "That is the stupidest, most ridiculous idea I've ever heard!" He stepped closer and scowled down at her. "You're running away, Toni," he accused flatly.

"I'm *not* running away." She denied the accusation with a desperation that clearly revealed the hypocrisy in her statement. She was too affected by his nearness to think straight.

Nick's eyes flashed and he caught her shoulders in his big hands.

If she hadn't been so distracted she could have evaded him, but the minute her body came up against his she was lost. Her slight frame molded itself to his muscular body with an intensity that belied every harsh word, every denial she'd ever uttered. Automatically she lifted her face. Her lids drifted down to half hide her eyes and her lips parted slightly.

Nick held her like that for a moment, searching her face. Their faces were only inches apart.

When he didn't kiss her immediately, Toni opened her eyes in puzzlement to look for any trace of contempt but desire was there instead. Surely he was going to kiss her. He had to; she wanted it so much.

"Why won't you be honest with yourself, Toni?" he murmured. His warm breath was on her parted lips and, without restraint, she raised herself on tiptoe to meet his lips. Her lips reached for him with a soft plea.

Instantly his mouth opened over hers. His arms came around to crush her in a tight embrace that Toni returned, clinging just as eloquently, just as greedily. Their tongues met in a clash of eroticism. The kiss they exchanged was not born of gentle emotion. It was a simmering, smoldering ember that had only been waiting to flame into spontaneous life.

One of Nick's hands twisted in her hair, bringing her head back, and the other curved over her hips bringing her into willing contact with his unmistakable arousal.

Toni's nails dug into the strong muscles of his shoulders. She pressed against him, wanting, needing to be closer. The blood in her veins sang gladly with the excitement, the biological urge to possess and be possessed by this man.

All of a sudden she found herself thrust away. They stood there, chests heaving, laboring for breath, and stared at each other in stunned confusion.

Nick recovered first. He turned away from her and raked his fingers through his hair. His hand swept down to the back of his neck, and he bent his head back to look heavenward with dazed eyes. "God!" he whispered hoarsely.

Toni's lips were trembling from the force, the unbridled hunger of the kiss. She wrapped her arms across herself and bowed her head, striving to control the shivering in her limbs.

When he spoke again she raised moist eyes to his profile. "You can't go," he said bluntly. There was still a trace of the struggle to keep his voice level.

"I'm going," she answered, but not because she was adamant about the trip. It was simply an automatic response to his attitude of command.

"Dammit, Toni!" he exploded.

Wincing inwardly, she went on as though he hadn't spoken. "I'm flying to Rome and I'll rent a car there. I paid for my plane ticket today."

The map of the Mediterranean might have been right in front of him for the speed with which he demanded incredulously, "Do you mean you're planning to drive through Yugoslavia and Turkey by yourself?" He sounded like he thought she'd lost her mind.

"Who said I was going alone?" she asked. Her question wouldn't have been so careless if she'd stopped to think.

Nick froze where he stood. His black eyes bored into her.

She knew the crime of her unguarded tongue. "Nick, I—"

"Forget it," he cut her off harshly. "I'm not going to ask who you're going with. It's none of my business. You made sure of that," he accused. "And to tell you the truth, I'm glad!"

Toni couldn't let this go on any longer. She couldn't stand for him to look at her as though he hated her, not after the kiss they had just shared. It was too meaningful, too profound, and answered too many questions. She had to try to talk to him, to tell him...but how? How could she reach him? "Nick, about last weekend. I—"

He interrupted grimly, "Forget last weekend, too. We both made a mistake that's all." An unpleasant laugh escaped from him. "A bad mistake!"

She certainly couldn't talk to him in this black mood. She'd just have to wait, and hope for another opportunity, but the silence between them was oppressive. "How is Angela?" she asked. The words were a weak attempt to inject some degree of normality into the atmosphere.

"She's fine. In fact, she's cheerful. Blanton, of course, stepped right into the breach."

She froze at the tone of his voice. He sounded... was he...? "Are...are you having regrets?"

"Regrets?" he questioned bitterly.

"I mean...." She had to get the words out. She *had* to know. "Regrets about your broken engagement?"

His eyes stabbed her like sharp pins. "Of all the things that have happened, that's probably the only one I *don't* have regrets about," he said in a low, very deliberate voice.

Toni tried not to let the overwhelming relief show on her face as she gathered all her courage for what she was about to say. Nervy was right, after all; it *had* to be said. Nick was as necessary to her as each breath she took. If she didn't try this one last time, she'd never know. She was leaving herself open to lifelong loneliness if he rejected her, but she had to take that chance. "I...I don't suppose it would matter to you now if, ah, if I said I'd changed my mind."

Something flared in his eyes, then was gone. He looked across at her coldly. "Well, well," he said, drawing the words out. "So you've changed your mind, have you?"

"Yes," she said softly. "Yes, I have. I want to marry you, Nick. I know you won't believe me, but I've done a lot of thinking this week, a lot of growing up, and I realize that you were right."

"It *is* rather hard to believe in light of your plans to travel," Nick said sarcastically. He studied her in silence, stretching the moment for what seemed like forever.

"Well, of course, I wouldn't go if...if...."

"That, my dear Toni, is a rather insidious form of blackmail."

Toni spun away from him. "Damn! I didn't *mean* it like that. You know I didn't!" she threw over her shoulder defensively.

"Didn't you?"

Slowly she turned back and lifted her eyes again. Her gaze pleaded for his understanding, but instead she was chilled to the bone by his lack of concern for her. Automatically she stood taller to face him and made a move to leave. She couldn't bear another second of this. If she stayed she would break down completely, and she refused to let him see her cry.

Nick reached out to clamp a hard hand on her shoulder, then dropped it abruptly. Couldn't he bear even to touch her? She looked at him steadily, hoping to discover some expression of a warmer emotion.

"Do you want to work for me as well?"

She hadn't even thought about that, but she answered automatically. "Of course."

He laughed, but the sound was not pleasant. "Of course. Now that you've had time to think it over you can see some advantages."

"No, Nick!" she denied frantically. He'd misunderstood again! She was really making a mess of this. What was wrong with her? In every other situation, with every other person, she was calm and collected. Only with Nick did she seem to fall utterly to pieces. "The job isn't important," she added with a tired sigh.

Suddenly he looked so disheartened, so disconsolate. His expression was harsh and weary. She questioned once more whether he could be hurting, too.

Then his eyes shifted to a point above her head. "Here comes Douglas." His eyes narrowed as they met hers again. "Suppose I think over your proposition and let you know tomorrow," he said as though he was considering buying a piece of property.

Toni swallowed. "All right," she murmured just as Douglas joined them.

Nick hesitated for a moment as though he was going to say something further, but then he turned to stride toward the parking lot. Toni and Douglas trailed after him, both lost in their own thoughts, their own fears.

Nick pulled into a parking spot a few doors from her building. He climbed out and opened her door.

Toni, who had commandeered the back seat, scooted forward to place her hand on Douglas's shoulder. "Try not to worry too much, Douglas. Nervy is in good hands."

The older man turned his head to smile at her and patted her fingers. "I know, Toni. Thank you for coming tonight. Minerva really liked those flowers."

"Good night, Douglas."

"Good night, Toni."

She slid out of the car to join Nick on the sidewalk. Everything had been said that could be said. Now she could only wait for his decision. Strange, that her whole life's happiness would be settled before long. It was almost with a feeling of peace, of gratitude that the matter was out of her hands, that she sighed.

Or was it? She had one more concession to offer. In fact, that concession had already been made in her heart during their conversation at the hospital. She might as well let him in on it now. They reached the bottom of the steps.

"I'm not going to Rome," she said softly. "You're right. It would be like running away." Judy was right, too, she thought. "I—I didn't want you to be bothered by it while you're making your decision. So, no matter what you decide, I'm not going."

"I think that's wise, Toni," he said quietly. "Good night." He watched her mount the steps and unlock the outside door. Just before she closed it securely she looked at him one more time. His hands rested casually on his hips while he waited to see her safely inside. He nodded abstractedly and walked away.

HOURS LATER Toni lay on her bed still dressed in the peach slacks and sweater, staring dry eyed at the ceiling.

It was too late. She had destroyed any feeling Nick had for her. Nervy said he loved her, but Nervy was mistaken. A profound sorrow made her heart heavy. She knew that he wouldn't marry her now. There had been no tender glow of love in his eyes when he looked at her. None at all.

The buzzer from downstairs jolted her out of her reverie. Who on earth? She looked at the clock on her bedside table. Three in the morning! Stumbling slightly, she made her way into the darkened living room and pushed the button on the intercom. "Who is it?" she asked.

"It's Nick. May I come up?"

Toni put a trembling hand to her temple. "Yes. Of course." Her fingers held the release for the door downstairs until she heard a click. Then she switched on a light and opened her door to stand there, waiting for the elevator to bring him up. What was he doing here at this time of night? Had he come to tell her that he wouldn't marry her? He probably wanted to get it over with. Blinking furiously to clear her eyes, she gripped the knob. If she could just live through these few minutes, she could live through anything.

When Nick approached her door she stepped back to let him in. He was still dressed in the well-fitting jeans. He had pulled on the blue cashmere sweater he'd worn the night he picked her up at Fridays. Remembering the softness under her fingers, she swallowed. Tonight he wore no shirt, and she could see the beginnings of the dark curly hair on his chest. The sleeves were pushed up casually over his muscular forearms. His physical presence was so substantial, in contrast to the dreams of him she had been living with, that she turned away nervously. "Would you like some coffee?" she asked.

He hesitated. "I won't be staying long."

Here it comes, she thought, so she spoke in a rush before he could say anything else. "Nick, I'm sorry about what I said earlier. It was presumptuous of me." Her back was still turned. She twisted her fingers together.

"Changing your mind again?" he asked in a scornful voice.

She spun around to meet his mocking eyes. The skeptical look there doused the flicker of hope in her, but she knew that she had to be truthful. She owed it to him. He would be perfectly justified in rejecting her as she had rejected him, and she owed him the opportunity. "No, I won't change again," she vowed, lifting her chin. "If you still want me, I'll marry you."

Nick thrust his hands into the pockets of his jeans, tightening the fabric over his flat stomach, but his face was still a study in indifference as he said, "Very well. We'll get married as soon as you graduate."

Her heart began to pound, her eyes glowed as she moved toward him, but at his next words she was turned to stone.

"But don't fool yourself that it's a marriage made in heaven, Toni," he said bluntly. "I fooled myself into believing that you were a different kind of girl, but I know better now."

"Then...then why, Nick?" she whispered.

He shrugged his broad shoulders. "It's time I settled down," he answered offhandedly. "I'd like a family. You're attractive and intelligent. You want something. I want something. Why not?"

Toni gasped.

"I do have a few stipulations. I think we need a prenuptial contract. Since I have some expertise in the field, I'll draw it up."

Toni didn't answer. She just looked at him numbly. A contract? She knew that a lot of couples had them now, but she had never thought that when she married she would have one. It seemed so cold, so cut-and-dried—a contract for love.

"I would like for us to be married here," he continued. "I'll make the arrangements for the day after your graduation. We can honeymoon at the house on the Cape. I don't think either of us wants to go through the mockery Agnes would insist on in Atlanta, do you?"

Toni shook her head, stunned by his nonchalant plans. The wedding didn't mean anything to him.

"When we return to Atlanta you can work for me. I'll make you the best damn contracts lawyer in the country *and* make provisions for your job if we split up."

She barely heard him as he went on in the same cold voice. "There are only a few other conditions. I'll draw up the contract and you can read it over."

She forced her voice through a raspy throat. "What if I don't like the terms?"

He shrugged. "I won't be unreasonable. The terms can be negotiated. One thing—I want Aunt Lydia to think that we are in love with each other; and another—if we have any children and the marriage ends, I want custody." His eyes pinned her. "Do you agree?"

Motionless before him, she found herself searching in vain for a brake in his firm expression. "It sounds so . . . so cold-blooded, as though anyone would do."

He interrupted sharply. "No! Not just anyone!" His eyes roamed over her, lingering on the full curve of her breasts under the sweater. For the first time since he had entered the apartment he touched her. His hand slid around the curve of her waist, and he pulled her slowly toward him until her thighs rested against his. His dark eyes flared.

She could hardly breathe.

"What do you expect, Toni? Vows of love? I still want you physically," Nick rasped. "The memory of your body, bathed in firelight, haunts me. I want you."

Despite herself, Toni swayed closer, offering herself for his kiss, and when it came it set off an explosion in both of them that could no longer be denied. She reached up, coiling her arms around his neck. His hands slid to cup her bottom, lifting her, molding her to the force of his desire. Their mouths were moist and hungry as their tongues met in a surge of passion.

Toni felt a thrill of triumph when Nick groaned her name.

"I missed you," he breathed into her mouth. "God! I never knew I could miss a woman so much!"

"I missed you, too," she whispered, then she gave a husky laugh. Nick was rapidly divesting her of her clothes. But with no deliberately slow seduction and none of the firm control he had shown at the Cape. Her sweater was pulled roughly over her head, her slacks unzipped and yanked down. He lifted her, strode blindly to the bedroom and dumped her on the white spread.

With any other lover she might have protested this impatience, but Nick was looking at her for the first time without that cold indifference, and it thrilled her heart to bursting. He still wanted her with a desperation that overcame all reason, and he could not hide it from her in a moment like this. Surely love could be rekindled where these strong emotions played. He stripped off his jeans and sweater with the same impatience, then Toni forgot everything in the heaven that was his arms. Their limbs tangled, their bodies clung until all too quickly they were transported to that other world where time and space were annihilated by flaming desire.

ROUSED FROM A LIGHT DOZE by a sudden chill, Toni rolled over, reaching for Nick, but the spot where he had lain was empty. She raised herself on her elbows, and his name was on her lips before she saw him.

He stood looking out of he window to the blackness beyond. His hands were thrust into the hip pockets of his jeans. The tension across his shoulders held them rigid. "I'm here," he answered. When he turned, the absence of expression on his face was the first thing she saw, and she felt her heart sink again. There was no hostility there, no self-abasement or regret, but that awful indifference was back. Toni could have stomped her foot and probably would have if she'd been standing up.

"I have to go," he said evenly. "My plane leaves early." She sat up, clutching the sheet across her bare breasts, but before she could speak he went on in that same hard voice, "I have some obligations that I have to fulfill before we can be married. It should take about a month," he said gruffly. "I want to be completely free for a long honeymoon on the Cape. I'll have my fill of your lovely body before we return to Atlanta."

Toni's chin came up defensively. "And what then, Nick? When you tire of me physically, what then?"

"It will all be spelled out in the contract. Unless you want to back out?"

That was impossible. Toni knew it the minute he'd touched her. Even if he hated her now she would take whatever he gave and hope that maybe someday.... "No, I won't back out. You can make any monetary designations you wish, but I would like one change in your contract proposal."

His eyes narrowed, "A condition, Toni?"

"Only one," she said with more confidence than she felt. "If the marriage should end because you fall in...in love with someone else—" she stumbled only slightly over the words "—I want uncontested custody of any children. I won't have another woman bring up my children!"

He looked at her. "All right, I'll agree to that," he said easily.

"Are you going to send me a copy?" she asked.

"That won't be necessary. I'll bring it when I return." His hands went to her nape. "And instead of a handshake...." His mouth came down, crushing hers briefly, before he let her go and strode to the door. "I'll see you in a month, Toni. Be ready."

She collapsed against the pillows after the door closed behind him. Her fingers went to her lips. The burning kiss had held no tenderness. Oh, God! What had she gotten herself into?

Nick called her from the airport early the next morning. "I wanted to let you know that I told Aunt Lydia. She was overjoyed. She would like for you to have dinner with her tonight."

"Certainly. Shall I call her?" she asked calmly.

"Please, and don't forget we are supposed to be madly in love!" He laughed, a discordant sound, and hung up.

THAT AFTERNOON Toni entered Nervy's hospital room with some trepidation. Nervy would easily see that something was amiss, and Toni didn't want her to worry.

Douglas had not yet arrived, and the old woman lay against the pillow with eyes closed, but when Toni would have backed quietly from the room she roused.

"Come in, child. I'm awake."

Toni moved closer to the bed and took her hand. "How are you feeling?" she asked quietly.

Nervy smiled. "Well, amazingly, even with all the sticking and prodding, I feel better."

And she looked better. Toni was relieved to see her skin had a healthy glow. Her eyes were clear and twinkled a bit when she said, "Sit down, Toni, and tell me your news."

"What news?" Toni was taken by surprise.

"Well it seems to me you've got lots of news," she mused. "I must say I'm not surprised. You always have had the good sense to take my advice."

"So you know?" Toni asked in a small voice.

"Nick called at lunchtime to tell me." Nervy chuckled. "He didn't know it was my idea."

Toni looked down at the hand she still held. "And what do you think?"

"I think it is wonderful if you love him as much as he loves you, Toni," Nervy answered very seriously.

Toni choked back a hysterical laugh. Nick must have decided that Nervy, as well as Aunt Lydia, should be convinced that they were very much in love, when in reality it was a marriage based on a callous contract. Toni forced what she hoped was a dreamy smile to her lips. "I adore him, Nervy," she said softly. "And we are going to be very happy." She didn't realize that Nervy had been holding her breath until the older woman let out a deep sigh.

Nervy smiled. "That's okay then. Have you told your father yet?"

"No. Nobody knows. Nick wants us to get married here right after graduation. He doesn't want the kind of wedding Agnes would think was proper and neither do I." Toni paused. "I'm not going to tell them yet, Nervy."

Sharp eyes bored into her. "Do you think that's a good idea?"

Toni dropped the hand she'd been holding and walked across the room to stare out the window.

"Maybe not. But I'd rather do it this way. I guess I'm just a coward."

"If there's one thing you're not, it's a coward!" Nervy remonstrated. "You're still feeling guilty, and you mustn't! I'll agree that if Angela had been head over heels in love with Nick, it would have been disastrous, but she wasn't and you know it! Now, honey, you must give him everything he would have missed if they had married without love."

"I hope I can, Nervy. I just hope I can, but I seemed to have made an unholy mess of things."

"What do you mean?" Nervy asked, her suspicions aroused.

Toni silently cursed her wayward tongue and hastened to reassure her. "Nothing at all! It will end well anyway," she said resolutely, but she wondered.

THE EVENING AT NICK'S AUNT'S was made a little more bearable because of the presence of Douglas. The two of them came from the hospital together in Toni's small car. Lydia welcomed Toni with open arms when they arrived at the house on Beacon Hill. Nick had certainly done a good job of convincing her evidently, for she didn't seem to notice that Toni was very quiet.

When the evening finally ended and Toni was leaving for her apartment, Lydia went with her to the door, her wheelchair whispering over the hardwood floors. She took Toni's hand in hers.

Toni could see tears sparkling on the long lashes.

"You've made Nick so very happy, Toni. He's like the son I could never have, and I knew he needed the softening influence of a special woman in his life. I'm so pleased that he found you."

Toni leaned down to hug the woman in the chair warmly. "Thank you, Lydia. I promise you that I'll do everything in my power to make him happy," she vowed.

10

Toni stood in front of her mirror and surveyed herself. The black gown and mortarboard made her look even paler, but the touch of dark red on the hood relieved the somberness a bit.

This afternoon her class was rehearsing for graduation, only a week away. Why did they have to rehearse, Toni wondered.

It was a waste of time. All they had to do was march across a stage, and her family wasn't coming anyway. Or at least she presumed they weren't since she hadn't heard from any of them.

For seven years she had looked forward to the event that would take place the next weekend, and now all she could do was wish it over.

She groaned and flung the mortarboard on the bed and took off the gown and hood. This should be the happiest time of her life. Graduation from law school and marriage to the man she loved should be milestones, but the only milestone she could remember was that day, almost a month ago, when Nick had left her apartment. He hadn't called since!

She could still feel the shaft of pain that went

through her at his harsh words: "Don't pretend it's a marriage made in heaven, Toni."

But it could have been! When she thought of the lovemaking that followed, she sighed. It had been wonderful until she'd awakened to find the mask back on Nick's face, as firmly in place as ever.

At least two things had turned out well. First, Nervy was much better. After a week of intensive testing the doctors had operated on her with complete success. Each day since the operation she had grown a little stronger, until now she was almost back to her normal self. Tomorrow she and Douglas were flying home to Atlanta. Toni almost wished she were going with them. She couldn't believe that she hadn't seen or heard from Nick since he'd left Boston three weeks and two days ago.

Except for one strange message—she had been visiting Nervy the day before yesterday when the doctor arrived. He was delighted to see her. It seemed he was a friend of Nick's, and Nick had asked him to do Toni's blood test for their marriage. He insisted on doing it then and there.

Toni and Nervy watched, openmouthed, as the man drew the blood from her arm. "Nick said he didn't want you to worry about anything. He'll take care of it all." Well, what did she expect? He had warned her. He didn't plan for her to share his life, only his bed. She had once thrown his love back in his face, and she would pay for it.

Toni had done some shopping. She brought everything to the hospital one day to show Nervy, and modeled the white silk sheath and the tiny wisp of a white hat. That was the day that Angela called Nervy's room. Vivacious and bubbling, she had announced over the phone that she and Jack were getting married. She spoke first to Nervy and then to Toni.

"Oh, Toni! Why didn't I see it? Why didn't I know? I almost made a horrible mistake, but now I'm so happy!"

Jack got on the line too. His jubilant tones matched Angela's. "Of course, Agnes doesn't think I'm up to Trabert's standards. You'd better latch on to him yourself, Toni. She'll die if she can't get him in the family." He laughed.

Toni almost told them then, but something, some fear, kept her from making her own announcement. Her hesitation earned a frown from Nervy and a raised brow from Douglas, but she silently shook her head.

The guilt feelings that Toni still harbored were totally unfounded, she knew now, but they would be a threat to any relationship, much less this cold-blooded marriage. She had to do something. That was when Toni first called Nick. She hoped if they could just talk...she longed to hear his voice. Maybe if she could convince him of her love he would thaw toward her and give her the reassurance she so desperately needed right now. She tried to call that night, but he didn't answer, so the next morning she called his office. Once she'd made up her mind to try, she couldn't wait another whole day to speak to him. She wanted to tell him simply that she loved him and missed him, and hope the admission would ease the bitterness between them before they were married. Was that a sign of weakness? No, she told herself. It took a lot of courage to make the call, she reasoned; it was a sign of strength.

Nick's secretary informed her that he was in California. No, she didn't know when he was expected back. He had been called in as cocounsel on a contracts case and it could take a week or more. Toni didn't leave a message.

She made herself wait a week, then she called again, hoping the girl wouldn't recognize her voice. But that hope was in vain. She had just missed him. He'd flown out the previous night to Washington. Would someone else be able to help her? No, no message.

One night, a few days later, she had studied late at the law library. She got off the elevator, her arms full of books, so exhausted that she could hardly put one foot in front of the other. The door to her apartment seemed miles away. Until she heard a faint telephone bell. Law books went sailing all over the hall. She sped to her door, pulling her keys from her pocketbook. Fumbling in her haste, she dropped them and muttered "damn" in frustration. It had to be him! No one else she knew would call this late. Finally she got the door open and raced for the phone. But all that greeted her was a dial tone. Cradling the receiver between her cheek and her shoulder, she thumbed through her telephone book and dialed his home number. He didn't answer.

She had taken to working herself to exhaustion every night so that she was asleep before her head touched the pillow. But there were other nights when she couldn't sleep, and those were the worst. Even so, she wouldn't consider backing out of the marriage, or the prenuptial contract, if that had to be a condition. She loved him wholly and completely, and she would marry him regardless. If he came to her apartment with a justice of the peace she would marry him. She would marry him in the middle of the night or in the middle of the street. She was his, and as long as there was the slightest glimmer of hope that they could regain what they had for such a brief moment that day at the Cape, she would try steadfastly. She would never waver again.

Professor Winter had called to her after class the week before. She'd been crossing the campus, heading for her car, but she stopped to wait for him. When he approached her, he suddenly switched from sober serious Professor Winter to jovially smiling John.

Toni returned the smile.

"Lydia and I were saying just the other night, my dear, that we'd like to see you again. She doesn't leave the house often, but, if I can persuade her, would you go out to dinner with us next Friday? We might go to Jimmy's down on the docks."

Toni hesitated.

"It would make us very happy to share an evening

with you before graduation and your wedding, my dear. Call it a graduation present, if you like."

Smiling, Toni thanked him. "I'd like that very much, Professor Winter."

"John, please, Toni. When we're not in class, that is."

Toni almost laughed out loud at her automatic switch back to the professor. "Certainly, sir," she assured him.

She began walking and he kept pace. "Speaking of class, Miss Grey, I'm a little disturbed at your performance over the past few weeks."

She looked at him, stricken. The blood drained from her face.

"My dear Toni, what have I said to put that look on your face?" John was back, and very alarmed that he had upset her. "It's not that serious, I assure you. You're too close to graduation with too fine a record for it to make any appreciable difference."

Toni started walking again, her head bowed. "I'm sorry, sir; I seem to overreact to everything these days."

"I only brought it up because it isn't like you, Toni. And because I want you to do well on the final exam." He was trying to reassure her.

"Thank you," she murmured.

John added tentatively, "I hope that godson of mine hasn't done anything to upset you."

Toni stiffened but kept walking. "Of course not," she said, but her eyes told a different story. She couldn't resist asking, "Have you heard from him lately?"

He laughed. "Not as often as you have, I'm sure! I have to leave you here. I will let you know what time Friday."

"Yes, I'll look forward to it. Goodbye."

And now it was Friday. There was the full dress rehearsal for graduation this afternoon and then the dinner tonight with John and Lydia to fill her day. The weekends were the emptiest times, but the next weekend wouldn't be empty. She would become first a lawyer, then a wife. She sighed. She had accepted Nick's proposal knowing he no longer loved her. She'd just have to live with it and hope that someday he would change. He had loved her once. Was it too much to hope his feelings would deepen again?

Toni didn't have a class this morning, so she decided to treat herself to breakfast at one of the outdoor cafés on Newbury Street. She slipped into a blue sun dress and sandals and strolled in the warm sunshine. She made herself put all worries out of her mind. So what if he hadn't called? She wasn't going to worry about that today.

It was a beautiful day, a day to treasure. In the middle of this bustling city, flowers and tulip trees bloomed in the tiny plots carefully guarded from the encroachment of concrete by quaint little wrought-iron fences.

The café Toni chose had gaily striped green-and-yellow umbrellas in the courtyard, and she found a seat at one of the tables. When the waiter had taken her order she sat back to enjoy the parade on the sidewalk a few feet away. Everyone said that Boston was a young person's town because of all the colleges and universities in the city or nearby, but today there was a potpourri of people strolling along the street. Young, old, in between; surburban matrons and conservatively clad businessmen rubbed shoulders with jean-clad students and colorfully dressed eccentrics.

Toni's mood was so positive that she decided to call Nick one more time. In her enthusiasm she couldn't wait until she got back to her apartment. There was a telephone just inside by the cash register. She left a generous tip for the waiter and headed for it.

The secretary was most concerned. "We have some very fine lawyers, Miss...." She hesitated waiting for Toni to fill in the name, but Toni didn't oblige her. "Can't someone else help you?" she asked.

"No thank you. Only Mr. Trabert will do, I'm afraid." *Only Mr. Trabert will do for me*, she silently added.

"Well, he left for Boston yesterday, and I'm not exactly sure when he will return."

Toni couldn't answer. She put down the telephone with a cold hand. He was in Boston, had been since yesterday and hadn't even bothered to call! Toni paid her bill and left the restaurant as quickly as her trembling legs would carry her.

When she arrived at her apartment it was only ten o'clock. The rehearsal was scheduled for two.

The walls seemed to close in on her. She had to get out of here. Moving numbly, she gathered up the cap and gown so that she wouldn't have to come back for them and left. She drove aimlessly away from the city out into the countryside. *Why*, she asked herself. If Nick's loneliness and impatience in any way at all matched her own, he couldn't have been in this city for five minutes without wanting to see her!

Tonight she was to have dinner with Lydia and John. Would he come along? He would be staying with his aunt, so it was a strong probability.

She didn't want to see him like that, she realized, surprised at her own anger. Not unless *he* made the effort this time. She had swallowed all pride when she proposed to him. Now it was time for him to make some kind of overture, and tagging along for a dinner engagement that had been arranged by someone else was no effort!

She stopped at a service station to use the telephone and dialed Lydia's number. When the older woman answered Toni took a breath and plunged in before she could change her mind. "Lydia, it's Toni. I called—"

"Toni! Where are you? Nick is here and he's been trying to find you."

Toni gave a wry smile. He hadn't tried very hard! "I'm studying," she lied. "And I'm afraid I won't be able to make dinner tonight. Please apologize to John for me, but I'm sure he'll understand with finals coming up next week."

"Toni! Wait!" Nick's strong voice came over the phone, but Toni hung up.

The rehearsal that afternoon took longer than was planned. Everyone was directed to the assigned seating areas and handed a list of instructions. The members of her study group were dispersed among the graduates, but Toni found herself seated in front of her friend Mary Ann. She twisted around and smiled.

"One more week and this will be for real!"

"Can you believe it?" Mary Ann grinned back.

Toni shook her head and the move set the tassel on her mortarboard swinging. She glanced at her watch and squirmed in her seat. When they were finally dismissed she didn't take time to remove the cap and gown but hurried across the campus to the parking lot.

She didn't see Nick until she was almost at her car, but suddenly there he was, coming toward her, looking as vigorous and masculine as ever. Maybe he was a bit thinner, she thought, as her eyes feasted hungrily on the sight of him. His navy blue sports coat was open over a white shirt and light tan slacks. His tie had been loosened.

"Toni!" he called and waved.

The sound of his voice jerked her out of the trance and reminded her of her anger. She whirled to jump into her car. She couldn't face him, not yet!

11

TONI GUNNED THE LITTLE CAR and left Nick racing towards the curb. Ignoring his shout to her to wait, she took the corner at twice the speed that was safe. She flicked off the mortarboard and flung it onto the seat beside her, then pulled the hood over her head. It landed on the seat, too. Her heavy mane of hair came loose from its coil, and the wind picked it up to fling it free.

In the rearview mirror she caught a glimpse of a taxi. Surely not! She couldn't be so unlucky! But shortly after she turned left onto CommAve, she could see in the rearview mirror that the taxi followed. There was no parking spot in front of her apartment, and she turned onto a side street. There was one! She parked, then not bothering to put the top up on her car, grabbed the keys, her purse and her mortarboard and hood.

Toni rounded the corner in time to see Nick get out of the taxi, and she started to run, the dark gown billowing behind her. If she could just beat him to the front door....

She was fumbling with her key and had the door open as he reached the steps. But it hadn't closed completely behind her before his hand was on it. She raced for the elevator and pushed the third-floor button. Were the automatic doors always this slow, she wondered frantically. Just before they were about to close, Nick's big hand came between them and they obligingly opened for him.

He loomed large over her cowering figure huddled in the corner. The doors closed behind him, and the elevator started up with a jerk. He took her shoulders in his strong hands and gave her a small shake. "Don't run from me!" he ordered sharply.

Toni was aware that he had only a slim hold on his temper, but he had no right to be so domineering. If he were going to treat her like an adversary then she would match his antagonism. She lifted her chin to a defiant angle. "Then let go of me," she demanded.

He shook her again, harder. "You crazy fool! You were driving like a bat out of hell! You could have been killed!"

"Well, it's no concern of yours! Oh, when will you leave me alone?" she wailed, twisting, trying to free herself from his unrelenting grasp.

"Never!" He let go of her and pivoted to the panel of buttons. His big hand slapped against it, hitting all four buttons at once, and the elevator shuddered to a halt.

There was a deathly silence for a moment. Then Toni came at him, fists flailing. "Damn you!"

He fended her off easily and sat her roughly on the floor in the corner. "Sit down!" he bellowed unnecessarily, since he had already made sure she was sitting. "Now, what the hell's going on with you?"

"How long have you been in Boston, Nick?" she demanded.

"Since yesterday. Did it bother you when I didn't call?" he asked sarcastically. He towered over her cringing figure, but fear and anger stiffened her backbone.

"Certainly not!"

A speculative gleam lit his eyes before his expression became inscrutable. He moved to the opposite corner of the elevator and sat down. His heavy breathing was loud in the silence. He massaged the back of his neck with one hand in a tired motion. Resting his arms loosely on his bent knees, he began to speak in a quiet voice. "I flew in yesterday and drove to the Cape to make sure everything was ready for our honeymoon. I didn't want to call you until I was sure I could make all the arrangements to marry you tonight!"

Toni wasn't sure she'd heard him right. Her eyes flew to his face before her chin dropped. "Tonight? But you said next week, after graduation."

"I know what I said. I changed my mind." He seemed to be holding himself in check.

"Wh—what about the contract?" she whispered, trying to gain time to sort out her thoughts. He assumed he could just come in and announce something like that!

He patted his breast pocket. "I have it right here," he said, watching her. "Are you going to sign it?"

His eyes were as black as midnight in his stiff face.

"And marry you tonight?"

"Yes, tonight!" His tone was adamant.

She wondered if there was any use to argue or if she even wanted to. "We...if...." She couldn't control her squeaky voice.

"Dammit, Toni! No conditions! Yes or no!" he flared.

Suddenly her temper sparked to meet his burning eyes. "I'm not one of your witnesses to cross-examine! Yes! If we ever get out of this stupid elevator!"

"You will?" The anger in his eyes began to fade, and color seeped into his ashen face. Slowly he sat up and moved toward her.

"Yes," she said firmly. "Yes, I want to." Her voice broke. "I'll sign anything! Anything you say! Oh, Nick, I love you so much!" She knew she was babbling, but she also knew that whatever he asked she would do. It didn't matter what the contract included. She would sign it, and she would marry him under any conditions he wanted to impose.

Nick took a deep breath, then let it out. "You'll never know how much I've longed to hear those words," he said with consummate relief. There was a suspicious glitter in his eyes. "I love you, Toni."

"You do? You really do? Oh, Nick, I was afraid I'd killed it all!" she wailed.

They reached for each other and met in the middle of the floor on their knees. Nick's arms were hard around her, his hands tangled in the tawny blond hair. He covered her face with kisses. "Don't cry, honey. I love you. God! Don't cry. It tears me to pieces."

"I'm not crying!" she sobbed against his chest. "But...oh, darling, I haven't stopped crying in my heart since you left." She hiccuped.

There are two ways to stop a woman's tears, and Nick took the most pleasant way. His mouth came down hard on hers, and she wiggled her arms free to wind them around his neck. They were lost in each other for a long time.

Eventually Nick sat back in his corner and pulled her onto his lap. He brushed her hair away from her face with a trembling hand. "Do you want to see the contract?" he asked, still shaken from the force of his passion. The hard stony look was gone forever.

Toni flinched in remembered pain. She pulled away from him slightly. "I guess so," she responded unenthusiastically.

Silently he took a folded document from his pocket.

Toni avoided his eyes as she took it from him, but he smiled down at her. Slowly she unfolded the stiff paper.

The contract was very short.

This agreement made between Nicholas Townsend Trabert, party of the first part, and Antonia Diane Grey, party of the second part, for and in consideration of the mutual love the parties have for each other, and

Whereas, the parties are desirous of establishing a home based on mutual trust, affection and a deep sustaining foundation for themselves and any future offspring,

It is therefore agreed that the parties will forever love one another, forsake all others and bond themselves to be eternally faithful.

Nick's signature was a bold slash on one of the two spaces at the bottom.

Toni caught her lower lip between her teeth to keep from laughing out loud in her joy and asked in a voice that grew stronger with each word, "Do you have a pen?"

He grinned down into the wide dusty-blue eyes and took one from his jacket pocket. She propped the paper on her knee and hastily scrawled her signature. Tossing the paper aside, she flung her arms around his neck. She got exactly the kind of response she wanted.

"But why tonight, Nick?" she asked after a long while. "You said next week."

"Two reasons, darling. One—I thought you'd want Nervy and Douglas to be here. They're leaving Boston tomorrow."

Her eyes sparkled. "Oh, yes! Yes, I do want them to be here!"

He looked down into her face tenderly. "And two— I simply can't wait another day for you. I've been working nonstop to finish all the business I had. When I left Boston, Toni, I didn't know whether or not we had a chance, but I wanted us to try, and the sooner the better."

"I called your office this morning," Toni told him. "Your secretary said you were in Boston, so I knew you were here, but when you didn't call...." She tried to hide her face. "I thought you'd given up on me."

His fingers gripped her chin to tilt her head up. His eyes moved lovingly over her features. "You called more than once, didn't you? My secretary said, 'a client kept calling.' She was worried. Rosie is a great judge of people's emotions from their voices, and she was sure there was something desperately wrong with that client. Why didn't you give her a message, you little idiot?"

"I think I was afraid to, Nick. If I had and you hadn't returned my call...." She shuddered.

Nick pulled her back into the warmth of his arms. He groaned, then murmured into her hair, "Darling, can you forgive me for being so cruel? When you told me the day on the Cape that you really didn't love me, it was like a white-hot sword in my gut. I guess I wanted you to hurt as much as I was hurting. God! I'm sorry!"

She curled her fingers around his nape to hold him closer. "I'm the one who should be apologizing. I know Agnes, you see. I think I realized from the beginning that she had talked Angela into the engagement!"

"You ought to have known anyway that I'd never give up on you, my darling. I love you. You're so much a part of me that my life is meaningless unless you share it." He kissed her deeply. "Don't you understand that yet?"

"Mine is, too, darling Nick," she whispered. Toni returned the kiss with all the sweetness that was in her.

Nick unzipped the front of the black robe. His head dipped to taste the delicious curve of her breast above the neckline of the sun dress. Then his hungry mouth returned to hers.

"I can't believe I'm not dreaming," she murmured when Nick finally let her take a breath.

He chuckled. "Neither of us is dreaming. You feel very real here in my arms. Although an elevator isn't the most comfortable place to make love."

Toni giggled and nestled closer to him. "I like it. You'll have to admit it's private."

Nick sobered. "There's only one more thing I have to say to you, sweetheart. I had dinner with your parents the other night. Angela and Jack asked me to be there for moral support. That was the night they told your parents they were getting married." He grinned wryly. "Jack didn't waste any time. And we've wasted too much!" His arms tightened. "I realized then that you hadn't told your family about us. I was furious with you. I was also deathly afraid you'd try to back out. So I told them myself. I was going to drag you to our wedding by the hair if that was the only way. But if you need your father to be here for this, darling, we can wait."

Toni lifted her hand to his cheek. "I think I was afraid to tell them—afraid you'd change your mind, but there is only one person I need, Nick," she whispered. Her eyes glowed radiantly. "Only one person who is absolutely necessary for my wedding."

She was rewarded with a hard kiss. "I hope your father will forgive us, but I can't wait any longer for you, my darling," he murmured against her lips. "By the way, they are all coming up next week for your graduation."

"Everyone?"

He nodded, but his attention was distracted. He released the zipper and slid the robe off, revealing the blue sun dress underneath. "I just hope they don't expect to be entertained," he told her in a thick husky voice. His hand slid up the silken skin of her back to burrow under the curtain of hair, while his lips traced a feverish path across her bare shoulders.

She felt the fires begin to ignite all the way to her toes. The feelings building in her couldn't be assuaged in an elevator.

They heard a commotion in the lobby below them, and John's gruff voice. "How long is this going to take?"

A muffled growl answered him.

"Do you mean I have to walk up all those steps?"

Toni jerked her head up in alarm and started to pull out of his arms. "It's John!"

Nick didn't release her. Instead he laughed and raised his voice. "Don't bother to walk up, John. We'll meet you at Lydia's as soon as the elevator is fixed."

"Nick, is that you?" John called.

"Yes."

"Have you seen Toni yet? Are all your, ah, difficulties worked out?" His booming voice was almost hesitant.

Toni looked at Nick with an accusing stare.

"Yes, John, she's here with me now."

"Stuck in an elevator! Oh, dear! I'm so sorry."

"Don't be! We're very comfortable." His hands caressed her breasts through the fabric of the sun dress. "Aren't we?" he whispered against her ear.

John's voice came up to them again. "I'll meet you then at Lydia's house. The man says it won't be much longer, so don't get too comfortable!" he chuckled.

Toni's face suffused with color. With her hands on his chest, she leaned away and glared up at him accusingly. "How did you arrange all this?" she asked, but her voice showed the effects of his kisses, his caresses.

Nick needed a steadying breath himself. "Well, I've talked to John once or twice. He mentioned that you seemed to be pining for something, and he was willing to help coordinate this meeting." He grinned.

"Why, that old fraud!"

"He thought it was for your own good," he teased.

Toni sighed. "I suppose I'll have to forgive him for interfering, won't I?"

"Definitely, my love. He was worried about how you would do on your final exams if you didn't straighten up!"

"I'm worried, too. Exams! Nick, my exams start Monday! We can't get married!"

"Oh, yes, we can! I'm going to help you study. As soon as we're free you are going to put on that white dress you bought. I understand you look very beautiful in it."

"You had Nervy in on this, too?" she exclaimed.

He continued, smiling. "And pack a bag with all your books and a very few clothes." He nuzzled her neck. Again his hands slid suggestively over her. "We'll go to Lydia's for the ceremony and afterward drive down to the Cape. I'll tutor you all weekend and have you back Monday morning. We'll stay in your apartment until after graduation. Then we'll go back to the Cape for a long honeymoon. How does that sound?"

"It sounds as though you were very sure of me! And it sounds like heaven. There's only one part of it that I'm concerned about."

"What part is that, my love?" he murmured against her soft skin.

"The part about your tutoring me," she said. Her eyes closed and her head fell back to allow him free access. "What sort of things will you tutor me in?"

His warm breath sent chills over her as he moved his mouth up her chin to find her lips. "Oh, a little of this, a little of that."

All of a sudden the elevator gave a lurch and smoothly began to rise. Toni extracted herself from Nick's arms and scrambled to her feet. Her face glowed as she watched him unfold his long frame to come up beside her. Her smile was exultant.

Steadying her with an arm around her waist, Nick said hoarsely, "Damn the man's efficiency."

Just as she swayed toward him the doors opened. Nick kept a firm hand on the protective rubber bumper while Toni gathered up the things that were scattered on the floor—her mortarboard and her hood, her purse and keys, the contract. She laughed. "It looks as if we've set up housekeeping in an elevator."

Nick chuckled. "It's better coming out than it was going in, isn't it?" he asked as he took her keys from her.

When she didn't answer for a moment he turned to look at her. Unbelievable happiness sparkled in her eyes.

Nick opened the apartment door and pulled her inside. He kicked the door shut behind them and his arms came around her. "If you keep looking at me like that we might never get to Lydia's." His mouth covered hers, electrifying every one of her senses. He kissed her deeply, passionately and then, with an immense effort, dragged his mouth away. "Oh, darling! I love you so much!"

Toni reached up a hand to touch his face. "And I love you, my darling. Forever."

He inhaled sharply and gave her one more brief kiss. "Forever might be too long in coming if we don't get you packed," he teased unsteadily and let her go. "How can I help?"

Toni simply stood there, looking at him, a blissful expression in her lovely eyes.

"Toni!" he warned.

She shook herself out of the enraptured trance and started toward the bedroom. "You can get my suitcase down from the shelf in the closet, if you don't mind." Suddenly she wanted to hurry. "I'll show you."

When Nick retrieved the case she grinned at him. "It must be nice to be able to reach that high without standing on a chair. You'll be handy to have around," she said pertly.

He laughed that deep laugh she loved. "Glad to be of service. Now get dressed, and pack that white thing I put you to bed in. I like that." He started back into the living room.

"But, Nick," she protested. "That gown isn't very honeymoonish."

He turned to cradle her face in his big hands. She caught her breath at the expression in his eyes. It was infinitely tender and loving.

"I've carried a picture of you in that gown around with me in my mind. You've never looked more beautiful or desirable." His lips worshiped hers for a moment before he pulled away. "Besides—it's the only one you'll need," he added in a husky murmur.

When Toni joined him in the living room a short while later, Nick was pulling books down from her shelves to add to a stack on the coffee table. He saw her out of a corner of his eye. "Just what I like, a woman who doesn't waste time." He turned with a book in his hand and froze. His eyes darkened and he took a deep breath. "Did I say you had never been more beautiful or desirable?" he asked hoarsely.

The fold of the white silk dress draped softly across her breasts. The fabric shimmered and flowed as she walked toward him. The tiny wisp of veil on the white hat was a halo around the tawny glory of her shining hair, and her long thick lashes framed the dusty-blue eyes so filled with love.

Nick dropped the book he had been holding onto the table with the others and reached for her carefully, as though she might disappear if he touched her.

Toni continued walking straight into his arms. They held each other for a moment, her arms wrapped around his waist, his encircling her shoulders.

Finally Nick gently unwound her arms—and reached into his pocket. "I almost forgot," he said, his voice a strangled whisper. "Give me your hand." He slipped a ring onto her finger.

It was a large blue sapphire, surrounded by sparkling diamonds.

"It's beautiful! Thank you, darling." Toni raised her head for his kiss, which was restrained, controlled only by the mightiest of will.

"Let's go," he groaned. "I'm in a colossal hurry to marry you."

Toni laughed. "Me, too."

They took the stairs.

THE TOASTING AT LYDIA'S HOUSE that night after the ceremony was jubilant. Toni bubbled and Nick glowed. The judge who married them was gracious and friendly.

When they finally said goodbye to everyone, John reminded Nick of his plans to tutor Toni. "Don't get sidetracked, now," he teased.

Nick's large warm hand covered Toni's small one. She turned hers up, and their fingers interlaced tightly as their eyes met and held.

"John, we've just entered into the most important contract of our lives. I promise we'll both study it very carefully."

THE AUTHOR

When Marion Smith Collins was seven years old, her prizewinning school essay was published in the local paper. Since then, she admits, "The thrill of seeing my words on a printed page has never faded." After selling her first romance novel, Marion realized that her true vocation was romance writing. "Now I've found my niche, my passion," she says. "I want to do this every day for the rest of my life."

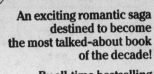